So...
∞
Volume Two

Alan D. Jones

Rising Sun Group Publishing

Atlanta, GA

Alan D. Jones/Rising Sun Group Publishing
www.alandjones.com

Book Layout © 2020 Alan D. Jones
Editing Services: L.M. Davis, Anika Jones & Alan Jones
Interior Page Layout & Design: Alan Jones
Front & Back Cover Design: Alan Jones

So... Volume Two/ Alan D. Jones. -- 1st ed.
ISBN 978-1-7344414-0-6

Rules of Engagement. Most of these stories are serials, meaning that new "episodes" will be released with each new volume.

CONTENTS

Hypnotized (No Worries)

V ery early on in our collective journey, on an easy, laidback Sunday, Cousin Kisha and I took up residence at our coffee shop, where it was not uncommon to find us posted up on Sunday afternoons. As we conversed, something flittered past our window. A moment later the front door of the shop swung open and in breezed a youngish looking brown skinned woman, with long, natural, braided hair, which fluttered as she moved. Her hair dangled slightly below her shoulders, with several of the beaded tips bouncing against her shoulder blades. As the place filled with late risers and the after-church crowd, most continued their conversations paying her entrance no mind, but I paused for a moment, as though I were hearing an alarm in the distance. There was a familiarity to the sensation I was feeling. Kisha, whose back was to the door skipped a beat too, her fork frozen for a moment midway between her plate and mouth, glancing over her shoulder as the tardy worker announced her apologies. These events took place before either Kisha or I knew who or what we really were, else, we'd have known not to ignore these signs when they're given.

Having shouted, "Sorry I'm late!" the woman moved, without waiting for a response, to her position behind the bar. New to us, but apparently known to the staff, she smiled generously, as she took up the lead baristas position.

A couple of minutes later, after working down a line of customers, the new barista stepped to our table, carrying a tray with small paper cups of tea, "Hi, my name is Simone. We're giving out free samples of a new tea line we're carrying. Please try some."

Both Kisha and I took one of the cups. The tea had a different taste, but we both liked it. But one thing did seem a bit odd at the time, in that the cups seemed to be bottomless. I mean it was just one small paper cup of tea for each of us, and yet, as I recall, we sipped from those cups seemingly all afternoon.

Later Simone returned to our table to inform us that we'd both just won an all-expenses paid trip to Panama, a promotional from the very same tea company whose tea we'd been enjoying all afternoon. She gave us instructions to get our tickets. I asked several questions, to which she offered in each instance a single answer, "No Worries."

The next thing I knew we were on our flight. Kisha was seated next to me, questioning the veracity of the prize. She commented repeatedly on how there had to be a catch. Among other things, Kisha was a human lie detector, so her words were more than some possible, cultural over sensitivity to being scammed (but then again, the streets say that, if you stay ready, you don't have to get ready).

Sitting on the aisle, I glanced back several times to see Simone sitting some ten rows behind us, smiling. Her lips moved, and though she was seated far behind me, I heard her voice, just as though she was seated right next to me. "No Worries…"

I recall landing, but I don't recall getting bags or anything. The next thing that I remember was the three of us, Simone, Kisha and me, sitting on a park bench somewhere downtown. It was an odd day, in that we were in Panama City, Panama, at 10:00 pm, and yet the sun was still shining brightly above us. Simone had sat us down apart from everyone else visiting the city park.

"Oh, oh, here it comes." A skeptical Kisha said leaning into me.

Simone smiled and spoke, almost sheepishly, "See, here's the thing. Someone stole something from me, a golden amulet. That amulet is the most important thing in the world and it must be returned to me. All I know is that the thief lives here. But there are millions of people living in Panama, and I don't know where to start. But that's where the two of you come in. You will help me find it."

"How so?" I asked.

"Oh, I don't know how it will be found, but I know who will find it. See, I know who you are, even if you don't yet know. And while, I would love to wait until that day when you know for yourselves who and what you are, I don't have, shall we say, the time for that. Suffice it to say that you, Blerd, are seer of the unseen, and knower of the unknown. While you, Kisha, though you don't know it yet, are an avenging angel.

"Okay..." I answered in a very drawn out way, unsure of just what she was trying to say. It was true that I had a knack for finding things, and always felt that in some other life, that I could have been a detective of some sort. But I certainly didn't see anything supernatural in those moments. Still, I didn't tarry too long on her point. Moving on, I asked her, "So, tell me, what happened?"

"Yes. Well, two days ago, several tourists from a cruise ship entered my shop in Kingston for a reading. There were five of them in all, and I read all but one them, one by one. After they left, everything seemed fine, until about an hour later, when my last customer for the day left. As soon as the door closed, I was flushed with a sense of terror of being incomplete. I knew that something was missing. Immediately, I ran behind the curtain which served as a barrier between where I did my business and my personal space. I began searching through my valuables. My credit cards were untouched, so were my rainy-day funds and my *go bag*, which had my passport and several gold coins, which I kept just in case I ever had to leave Jamaica in a hurry. But then, lastly, I looked under my mattress, searching for my amulet. It was the most important thing of all my possessions, and it was gone. I ran out into the street, searching among the long shadows, and saw nothing. But then a realization came upon me. Given that the amulet was hidden under my mattress on the side opposite from the side of the bed on which I slept, I realized that this was no regular opportunist, who would have rummaged through my private space, while I was distracted doing my readings. I was targeted. And as I thought on it, my spirit told to me that he was not truly associated with the other men, beyond being a passenger on that cruise ship. I discovered that the particular cruise ship in question originated from Panama. And that's why I'm starting my search here."

I thought for a moment and then asked, "Do you have a map of Panama?"

Simone pulled a map of Panama from her purse, unfolded it and then handed it to me. Initially, I was unable to focus because of the question which still lingered in my mind, that demanded an answer. I blurted out, "If it's nearly midnight, why is the sun is still out?"

"That's a meaningless question. In the end what does it matter? Focus on the task at hand. No Worries, right?" Simone replied back as she pointed again towards the map.

I replied back, "Right, no worries..." I turned the map back and forth in such a way that I could take it all in. As I settled into position to see the entire map, I placed my index finger on a small town in northwestern Panama. And then I just knew. "Your amulet is here," and I pointed towards the map.

We hopped on a bus headed out of town. It was only then that I recognized the rhythmic stride of a metronome, in the background marking off time, framing existence into a common language that we all share.

But in that moment, I thought, "What if existence is not at all what we believe it to be?" What if in truth, on a quantum level, we are extradimensional beings having a temporal experience? What if our consciousness is merely a part of a greater whole, which we can never see in the flesh, no more than an individual neuron can perceive a little girl jumping rope? And what if our consciousness is the only part of us which is truly eternal, a part of some grand all-knowing collective, which we in the flesh can never perceive?

And what if all of our perceptions of time are flawed, flaws to which we've conformed so that we, the *neurons,* might have self-relevance? And what if all our measures of time are delineations which only have relevance within the space we occupy at any given moment, be they ticks of a clock, measures on a page or the vibrations of an atom (perhaps even a lifetime)? Thus, as spatially confined beings, from our perspective Time presents as some immortal being, which we can never overcome. But in truth, from that higher plane, that higher dimension, all the events of our lives are like words on a page, where the letters become increasingly smaller as they reach the end of each page, so much so that every story, every chapter in the book of existence ends in a shared singularity. From the higher plane, all is already written, and time is nothing more than a line on a page. And through quantum entanglement might we not read ahead into the next chapter, and know things we, the neurons, ought not know? Taking these thoughts in whole, a realization struck me like a lightning bolt! What if...

Just as I was on the verge of the Holy Grail (a unified field theorem), Simone snapped her fingers in front of my face and I returned to the present state. She uttered under her breath, "Hash tag, side effects." Then, she announced to us as she stood up, "Come on, this is our stop, the town you pointed to on the map."

We stepped off the bus and into a town of empty streets. And while my watch stated that it was 2 AM in the morning, the sun was so bright that I had to shield my eyes. Seemingly involuntarily, I spoke, "Yes, this is it. This is the place. Follow me."

I led the three of us out of the town center, down a dirt road and into the country side. As we proceeded, every so often, when the road forked, Simone would whisper within my hearing, "Trust yourself."

Unprompted, Kisha added, "It is true cousin. You are seldom, if ever wrong about such things. You are truly gifted."

It was nearly five in the morning when we reached our destination, and yet the noonday sun illuminated the small gray hut I sought like some golden treasure. "Here." I announced.

Cousin Kisha pulled an arrow from her quiver, and placed it in her bow, setting her sights on the front door of the shack. She'd trained as a sniper in the army, but took up bow hunting once she returned to Georgia. She'd met a Georgia boy overseas, and they continued so when they returned home. He even took her out bowhunting for deer. But something about being from the south, still to this very day, creates a strong headwind against interracial relationships, which cannot be ignored. Although, as Kisha likes to tell it, she gave back the flannel, but kept the bow. She steadied her breathing as she leveled that bow towards the front door.

I checked the door, and found it to be unlocked. I glanced back at Simone and she nodded for me to proceed. But as I began to pull the door open, a large brown bear roared through it, knocking me to the ground, as it ran towards Simone who'd been standing ten to fifteen feet behind me. Then from the darkness an arrow struck the bear in its front shoulder. In anger the bear rose up on its hind legs above Simone, who'd also fallen to the ground along the walkway.

But before the beast could land a killing blow upon Simone, a second arrow from Kisha pierced its right eye. The beast immediately fell to the ground, crying out in pain.

Composing herself as she attempted to stand, Simone lifted her hand towards the injured bear, repeating over and over, "Spirit of the bear, leave this man and return to your home. He is unworthy of your presence." With each recitation, the beast transformed, becoming smaller and smaller, and with each iteration, more and more human, until at last, it was.

While Simone moved quickly into the fallen man's home, I knelt down over our naked opponent and felt for a pulse. I found a weak one. As he reverted to human, the transformation and reduction in size caused both arrows to recede from his flesh. And yet, he lay there like a dying animal.

Moments later, Simone returned from the sad looking shack, shouting, "I found it...!!!" as she held aloft the shining metal and bejeweled amulet. She was obviously pleased with herself. When Simone reached us, she handed the amulet to Kisha. Immediately, the object began to glow in her touch, as brightly as the noon day sun.

"What is it?" asked Cousin Kisha.

As Kisha handed the object back to Simone, the spellcaster replied, "Let's just call it a gateway for now. But one day, not so long from now, you'll know all too well, what it is." Simone strung the amulet around her neck, hiding it under her blouse.

When Simone turned towards me, I asked, "What about him?" pointing at the naked man lying in the walkway.

"When he transformed, the arrowheads fell from his flesh. So, as the world sees it, there's nothing wrong with him. But metaphysically, he's hovering just outside of Eternity's door. There's nothing that modern medicine can do for him. Now, it's simply a matter of his own will and his own spirit. But that being said, him still being alive, is a problem; for I know that if he recovers, he will come at me again. If I were smart, as the world sees it, I would kill him where he lay. And yet, I cannot, for that is not who I am. So, I'm trusting the universe in this matter. My path does not allow me to do harm to the defenseless."

As we began our long trek back to town, Simone offered a seemingly random comment towards Kisha, "… and when you come into your own, your essence will be able to move from plane to plane as easily as others walk across a room. At that time, you'll be more powerful than me, in fact, you both will be in that day." It was in that moment, in the 3:00 AM sun, that I realized that Simone was actually Voodoo Priestess, the Jamaican contractor we'd enlisted in one of our earliest adventures. I'd seen her the entire time, and yet, still not had not seen her at all!

With that realization, I awakened in my own bed, with a start. I looked all around me, feeling displaced and out of sorts. As I stumbled to my feet, I nearly tripped over my clothes from the previous evening. Reaching the bathroom, I noticed that my eyes were severely bloodshot, but I pushed through the moment and readied myself for work.

On my way to the train station, I stopped to pick up a cup of coffee. Grabbing my order, I turned towards the exit door, and saw Cousin Kisha walking in. "Kisha!" I called out. I saw that her eyes were bloodshot too. After a quick hug, I nearly shouted to my cousin, and true sister in this life, "Kisha, I had this dream last night…"

Kisha interrupted me, "Did it start here, at that table over there, against the window and…"

I jumped back in, "and ended in Panama?"

Kisha nodded.

I thought for a moment, and whispered, "The tea."

"The damn tea…" Kisha replied.

We both dropped our heads and I conceded, "Voodoo Priestess."

Kisha shook her head and replied soberly, "That heifer…"

Next: Let Me In

Let Me In...

Ten years into the life of this well intentioned collective of ours, we'd gone more than a week, without hearing from Oliver, aka Money. His spontaneously being gone for long stretches of time wasn't unusual, since Money often accompanied his rich and wealthy friends on their excursions. But since he'd became a part of our collective, he'd always checked in with one of us before taking off. Right off, in my spirit, I knew something was wrong.

Marketing Girl knew several of Money's friends, and reached out to them to see if they'd heard from him. None had. And yet we moved as though there was still hope, for in Money's sphere of wealth and affluence, he had friends who would allow him to stay in their well-placed condos and homes around the world; be it a large two bedroom across from Central Park, a cabin in Aspen or a studio apartment in San Francisco's Fisherman's Wharf. Money was blessed to have a trust fund, which could indefinitely support his basic living expenses as long as his annual withdrawals remained below four percent of his trust. It wasn't fancy Mediterranean yacht money, but technically, he didn't need to work. But he did so for his own sense of self-worth, and it was expected within his realm not to be an unapologetic *loafer* (vestiges of the whole Puritan *work is good* ethic, which morphed in the 1980's into wealth is virtue). We all knew that his path and internal drive were far different from us mere mortals. Money, was clearly a fallen angel from Elysium, who'd chosen to bless us with his presence. And yet...

Money's parents opened a missing person's report with the Atlanta Police Department and granted us access to his condo, once the police were done with the place. Money's twin sister, Rose, joined us at the condo for the property manager to let us in (and no, it was not lost on me, that Money's parents had named him Oliver and his twin sister Rose, like in the classic Oliver Twist novel).

"So sorry about all of this. He seemed like such a nice guy," the property manager commented as he let us in.

I took his words within the kindness in which I knew they were offered, but Rose glared towards him in a way that gave me chills. The manager got the non-verbal message and backed out leaving us alone. Then as soon as the property manager pulled the door close behind him, Rose broke down. Then, so did Marketing Girl, followed by Kisha and Grimes. I didn't cry, not because I'm such a badass, but rather because of my own brokenness. If I could have shed a tear, I would have. But that's a story for another day, this day's story is about Money.

In that moment my mind drifted back to the last time I had dinner with Money. We met at his favorite steak restaurant on Peachtree, just south of Lenox Square mall. Money ordered a bottle of their finest blackberry brandy. I don't really drink, but he knew that I'd have at least half a glass with him. After we'd placed our orders, Money said with a smile, "Blerd, how goes it my man?"

"It's your world, brother. You tell me." I said with a nod to the disparate worlds in which we moved.

"Better than I deserve, far better than I deserve…" his voice faded out as he lifted his glass to his lips. I nodded in response. In that moment we both acknowledged what we both knew, but never spoke of. I'm good at keeping the secretes of my friends. Money broke the quietness between us, "You know Kisha read me the moment she met me, even if she didn't know any specifics regarding the things I've done, she knew who I was."

"We all have a past." I offered in my familiar role of mediator.

"Yes, we do. But what Kisha sensed, you, given your gifts, have come to know in detail over the years. Yet you've never said a word."

"Why would I?" I tilted my head and took my first sip.

In the condo, once we'd composed ourselves, I made a suggestion. "I'm sure that the police are tracking his phone and I know that they scoured this place for clues. But, …"

"But…?" Kisha replied

"I was able to get into Money's online calendar and saw that he was due to be at a meetup Saturday before last. Looks like it was one of those popup events that rich folks do, where they charter a flight, and all they tell you, is what to bring, and you find out the destination only once you land. Now, while I'm not familiar with Money's wardrobe, I'm hoping that one of you is. If we can figure out what he took, maybe we'll have a clue as to where he might have gone. Maybe that will give us some idea of where he may have gone."

While I continued my online search for clues, Rose and Marketing Girl started in Money's bedroom closet, while Kisha searched his hall closet by the front door. With a quickness Kisha called out, "His heavy winter coat is gone!"

From the master bedroom, Marketing Girl answered back, "And so are his favorite sweaters."

I answered, "The local office for the travel agency planning the trip is in Buckhead. If we can get a listing of charter flights they sent out that Saturday, maybe it will tell us something." Their office was about a ten-minute drive from Money's condo.

So, we all hopped into our cars intent on paying the agency a visit. Rose rode with me. As soon as we pulled off, she asked. "Do you think he's alive?"

"I'd like to think so."

Rose sat in silence for a full two minutes, as we rode. Then still looking out the closed passenger window, Rose spoke, "So, how much do you know about Money's life before he connected with all of you?"

I paused a beat before replying to her as kindly, as I knew how, "Not a whole lot."

"But...?" Rose turned towards me, expectantly.

"I sensed that he had a past that he didn't want to talk about, so I let it be. I guess, I really didn't want to know."

"None of us did." Rose replied. Then after pausing for several breaths of deliberation, she continued. "Before his pivot, most would argue that my brother spent his days doing what attractive men with money do. But it was more than that; what my dear brother enjoyed most, sadly, was breaking people. Truth be told, he was an emotional sadist. But as a family, we chose not to see what he'd become. Nana had heard whispers from her friends, but had always deferred to our parents to address the matter. But they never did. They rationalized their golden boy's behavior, *it's not like he's raping anyone*, they'd say. It wasn't until Nana, knowing her days were short, called him home and confronted him regarding the life he was leading, that something changed. I was at the door listening, and while I couldn't hear everything she said to him, I will never forget what she said at the end. She kept repeating, as they both cried, "I raised you better than this..."

It wasn't terribly long after that, that he connected with you all." I'd known that due to their parent's professional pursuits, Nana had done most of the day to day parenting of Rose and Oliver. Rose continued, "The person he'd become broke her heart. And though Nana had a poor prognosis at the time, we all know that she lost her will to live on that day. Since then he's tried his best to make up for all the harm he did, by helping others. I don't know if it works that way, but what choice did he have?"

Though I knew that she expected me to be shocked by her revelation, I merely nodded and held my silence, knowing that the truth was a bit more complicated than that. In truth, there had been hints all along the way, since I first met Money. The awkward pauses on the very rare occasion, when we encountered people from his past. He'd moved to Atlanta in part, to get away from his past. But you never know when your past will walk through the gates of Hartsfield-Jackson International.

Money carried a weight which he refused to share with the us, no matter how often we offered. More specifically, he refused to let me in, the one earthly soul who could have best helped him. But then was not the time to recount my efforts to share her brother's burden.

A moment later, the former Catholic school girl, reengaged me as she rubbed the cross hanging from her neck between her fingers, "Do you think he did enough? Enough, to outweigh the things he did before?"

Noting the tear creeping down her cheek, I shook my head, "I don't know about that. I would think that such an evaluation is less a score card, and more of a narrative, where the ending matters."

As we drove on and Rose mulled over my assessment, my mind drifted once again to my last dinner with Money.

"So, when did you know, know who you really were?" I asked.

"I'd thought about such things for a long time, but never acted on them. That is until my tenth-grade year. My mentor at the time, whom my parents had found for the specific purpose of exposing me to the real world, spent time with me while my parents were out conquering the world for the sake of the capitalist gods they served.

He allowed me to shadow him after class and on weekends. He owned several meat and potato businesses in the black part of town. On one of these excursions he catches me palming a couple of Hostess Cupcakes from a bodega we'd stepped into. After making me apologize to the owner, he hauled me off to a furniture store he owned. He took me to the storeroom and tells he was going to have one of his evening storeroom guys sort all of the furniture in it, but decided that I should have the honor. He tells me that he'll be back at five to pick me up. Mind you it's May, and the storeroom is not air conditioned, and it's just me. I'd never worked so hard in my life. He returns at five pm sharp to retrieve me. He explains that he wanted me to see how hard the average Joe works, often for minimum wage, and how it's just wrong to steal from them. But that wasn't the lesson I got. I seduced his daughter the next day. In that moment, I knew exactly, who I was.

As I pulled into a parking space at a coffee house around the corner from the travel agency, Rose finally replied, "I surely hope you're right."

Rose stood upon the only hope she had as she exited my car. Kisha, Grimes and Marketing Girl rolled into the parking lot and exited their vehicle.

Rose leaned towards me and offered softly, "I really want to believe that he'd turned a corner."

It was in that moment that I remembered how Rose had spent much of her life cleaning up after her twin brother. Wrapping my arm around her shoulder, I replied "And he had..." as I tried to comfort her.

"And yet the bill still comes due, Huh? This is all so unreal..." She said as she pulled away and the others met us on the sidewalk.

Standing in a loose circle, Rose asked, "Please tell me again, what am I doing?"

I answered, "Okay, here's the deal, if there is something nefarious going on, we don't want whoever is behind Money's disappearance to know that we're on to them. So, we're going to send you around the corner to the travel agency with a hidden mic, of course. But you'll also be carrying this special pen in your purse. It's a special type of wireless router that will allow me to access to their Wi-Fi network signal. If I can access their network, maybe I can confirm that Money did fly out and where he may have gone. Just leave it anywhere. We'll be in this coffee shop waiting for you."

Rose departed on her mission, but I already knew that we'd never see Money alive again. There were too many tell-tale signs to think otherwise. No ransom note, no contact for over week and a trail wiped clean, which showed intent. In truth, not only did I already know full well that Money was dead, I also knew who was behind it. Cousin Kisha knew it too. Even Marketing Girl, who held out hope and never revealed her doubts to Rose, knew that the odds were long. Only Grimes believed that Money was still alive, but he was someone who'd never found a grain, he couldn't go against. But as for Rose, I knew that she needed this, thus I played my part. As Rose strolled down the street and towards her target, my thoughts returned to my last supper with Money.

"So, was that it? Or did something else happen which brought you to us?" I asked Money.

"Well, I told you about how my Grandmother scolded me, right before she passed away, but there's more to the story. At that same time, I was dealing with this couple off and on, that I'd met at a swingers weekend thing. And unwise as it was, we continued to hook up. That's not how that's done in the lifestyle, and yet we did. They'd

plan some destination vacation, and I'd get a ticket in my inbox. I was down, because I was still of a mind that I could get by simply dialing things back a bit, you know? But on the real, I knew that they were both in love with me, which in the past had been like a secret badge of honor that I wore beneath my clothes. My own pride seduced me, as it always did, and I held on to that part of my old self. The more they cried and pleaded, the bigger the rush for me... until that day. The day, he called me every thirty minutes or so, begging to see me. I ignored his calls, as I'd ignored so many calls, from so many over the years. Then about seven pm, I get a call from a friend of my father who was also a swinger, who knew Pete. He said to me, hey, Pete jumped off a building today. My father's friend was then silent as I listened to him breathe, before hanging up. Death is a bell which cannot be un-rung.

A few days later, I went into the office, not because I had a meeting or anything, but simply because I didn't want to be alone. At nine fifty-nine AM, Pete's wife strolled into the brokerage, slapped me in the face and spat on me. I didn't say a word, I didn't call the police or even security. It was then that I realized that I needed to make a clean and complete break from my old life. I legally changed my first name and moved to Atlanta. The only part of my old life that I kept were my parents and my sister. And though I still like to do my thing, I don't prey on fragile people, in fact, I avoid them. And I know that there are some places, figuratively and literally, that I can never go again. For me, it was an addiction. I can never go to that place again."

"And Pete's wife?" I asked.

"I've not seen her since. Though from time to time, I do look her up on social media."

I nodded in acknowledgement. Ironically, now that Money was actually someone who gave a damn, he realized that even were he to attempt to reach out to offer some sort of apology, he'd cause even more injury. In truth he was powerless to sooth her pain. Some things, you simply cannot fix in this earthly plane.

As the dinner continued on, he shared more of his misadventures. Not in a gratuitous way, nor was he bragging. I was no priest, but he felt the need to confess his sins to someone, and that night I was that someone. Some of what he told me, I already knew. It's my gift to know things, and anything relevant to one of our cases, I knew already. And yet I sensed that he was holding back, and for once, I invaded Money's emotional space. As we waited on the bill, I said, "Dude, I appreciate you sharing all of this with me this evening, but I get the feeling that something else is on your mind."

Money paused considering the moment. Then he smiled, "In due time you'll know it all. Just promise me this, please keep my sister away from all of this. You know how she is, so this is not an easy ask."

I knew well what he meant. I knew his sister, and she'd want to rescue Money, as she'd done so many times before. To her credit, she's not the kind to give up. In that one respect, we're very much the same. Tenacity was her fatal flaw, as it was mine.

But we'd made some powerful enemies, ones who played for keeps. Many a time I could delved into Money's past, but I'd chosen long before never to pry into whatever secrets my teammates might have. And at the end of day, we're each captains of our own ships, so I simply replied to him, "Sure, I'll make sure that she's safe."

I looked up to see Rose eagerly returning to the coffee shop. Excited she said a bit too loudly, given the nature of what we were doing, "So, did it work?"

I assured her, "Yep, but it's going to take a while. But this was a big help." Less than twenty minutes later, we were all out the door. That evening I took Rose back to the airport.

A week or so later I forwarded an online news story from the AJC, our local Atlanta newspaper, which detailed how the travel agency was busted for laundering money for a major drug cartel. Soon after, remains were found beneath the cartel's stash house. Each had been shot in the head, burned beyond recognition, and their teeth removed. I allowed Rose to believe that her brother was one of those unknown victims.

The day after I tied a bow around the whole Rose situation, when I told, Kisha, Marketing Girl, Grimes and few of our contractors, what I'd done and why I'd done it. In my investigations of other cases, I'd come across this particular "travel agency" several times and realized that they were dirty, and connected to some heavy weight baddies. So, when Rose demanded to come down to Atlanta for herself, to somehow accomplish what the police and Feds could not, Money's final request came to my mind, and I made it so.

At first, my crew was upset with how I'd chosen to handle things, setting up this elaborate charade, but after I explained that it was Money's final request, that his sister not be pulled into all of this, they understood. And they knew that I'd do the same for each of them. And yet, these events made two things very clear. One, we all needed to leave Atlanta. Secondly, we could no longer wear the blinders of willful ignorance. Entropy was actively pursuing the painful demise of each of us. This was the truth of things, harsh as it was.

The truth of the matter was that Money was indeed dead, and murdered at the hands Entropy. He'd been brutally tortured and his body dismembered, with many of his limbs removed while he was still alive. I knew this because his executioners filmed the event and posted it on a snuff site. A facial recognition program I was running had found the footage. Such things you cannot un-see, and now, in times when those images come to mind, a feeling sweeps over me. It's a knowing that I could have helped him, if only he had let me in.

Epilogue: About three weeks after Money's memorial service, I received a letter from the executor of Money's estate. Money had made me the executor of his trust. The letter also contained Money's last words to me, "You know what to do...". Dude had found a way to live on...

...Meaning, I'd been working on a cloud based A.I. (artificial intelligence) project and I can't quantify just how much of an impact the funds from Money's trust made. But I can say that I would not have finished as soon as I did without the four percent, I withdrew from the trust each year forward. And as things turned out, having it done sooner than later, would be far more critical than I could have ever imagined. In fact, even as we were still grieving Money, the Universe was busy acquiring other pieces that I didn't even know we would need.

Next: *The Zealot & The Heretic* (or what Marketing Girl calls *No Way in Hell*)

The Zealot and The Heretic

66"Mark it." The Zealot called to the Heretic.

After calling out the latitude and longitude of the mark, the Heretic replied to the Zealot, before going on, "So, you don't like these missions that Blerd sends us on?"

"Well, I can't say that I don't like them. I'm just saying, that he tends to feed us the side dishes, while he keeps the main courses for himself. Money was just murdered, and he has us up here in the frozen tundra on a snipe hunt." The Zealot, a former special forces Marine, lamented.

As the Zealot marched on through the snow, with his eyes affixed to the sonic imaging device he held between his two hands, the Heretic, an ex-Intelligence officer who served time for releasing classified information held by various governments around the world, followed with handheld GPS mapping device. "I hear you. But have you ever thought that maybe he's protecting us?"

"Oh, I know he is!" the Zealot laughed, "Blerd only pulls people into his inner circle, when there's no other choice."

"But everyone in the inner circle has a price on their head. So...?"

"It's just who I am. I'm the Zealot, if I'm in, I'm in! I don't really know how to be half in."

"Yeah, there's nothing worse than being half in."

"Really?

"Hey, I got a joke for you. *A Zealot and a Heretic arrive at the pearly gates together, car crash or some such foolishness.*

Anyway, St. Peter, says 'Welcome Zealot. Come right in.' The Zealot smiles assured of his place in the hereafter, and he steps right through the pearly gates. Then St. Peter turns to the Heretic and says, "Welcome Heretic. Come right in."

The Zealot shouts, "Hold up! He's getting in too?"

"Yes..." St. Peter says.

An obviously disturbed Zealot, pitches a fit, "Oh, hell no! If the Heretic is here, this place can't be all that, what's the other place look like?"

The Zealot offered only a sigh and walked on through the white powder, as the snow continued to fall. The Heretic loved to tease and challenge the Zealot, but he had mad respect for him for the price he'd paid for integrity's sake. The Zealot was a commissioned Special Forces officer, serving in one of the many off book wars in Africa, when he heard a visiting general demand that aerial ordinance be dropped on a village, where he believed insurgents to be, despite the large number of civilians living there. The general, not realizing that the Zealot was a man of color, justified the strike by saying, "It's not like we're dropping bombs on Evanston Indiana. No one really cares what happens to *these* people." Later, the Zealot reported the general for committing a war crime. The general lost a star, but the Zealot lost a career. The Heretic didn't see eye to eye with the Zealot on many things, but he knew without doubt that he was a man of honor, and would forever have his respect, regardless of how many verbal jabs, he tossed his way. So, he smiled quietly, knowing that the Zealot's non-response, was all the response he needed from his comrade.

Minutes later the Zealot called out again, "Mark it."

The Heretic does as the Zealot asks, but can't help but comment, "Wow, whatever's down there, is huge."

"Yep, this my friend is most definitely not a snipe hunt. Blerd's source is legit."

The Heretic was silent for a moment or two as they proceeded, before posing a simple question "The Alchemist?"

"Perhaps, assuming that he, she or they actually exist." The Zealot replied before going on. "You're the hacker, you tell me."

"Well, when you don't want to sound crazy online, you go with the premise that the Alchemist is a collective of hackers who intervene on behalf of those in need against the powers that be."

"But..."

"But when speaking in real life, one to another, none of us is really sure who or what the Alchemist is. And here today, in this moment, I'm even less sure."

The Zealot stopped to show the Heretic the image on his screen, which at that point displayed an entire image of the object below the melting glacier, "Especially, when you're staring at the image of an alien spacecraft buried far beneath the artic ice."

"True Dat... I guess we're in the inner circle now, huh?" The Heretic was silent for a long moment, weighing his next words carefully, "So..., what now? I mean I guess, we should go back to town and head home tomorrow morning with our findings..."

The Zealot shook his head, "But...?"

"But that don't sound right. Surely, the universe did not bring us to a real-life alien space craft to simply take an ultra sound image of it and then go home. I think we can both say with absolute certainty that we, neither figuratively nor literally, will ever pass this way again!"

"Dude, that's not our mission. Going off mission is how things go wrong. Besides, that craft is hundreds of yards below us, and there's no way that we can get down there."

"But what if I told you, there was a way that we could?"

"I'd say at long last; your dreads have finally gotten the best of you."

"Give me two days. That's all I ask."

"Really?"

"Bruh, you know me."

Not believing his cohort would be successful, the Zealot relented. "Alright. Two days.

"Alright, alright... Besides, it would be a shame to come this far and not experience the town. Your racially ambiguous behind will fit right in."

"Don't laugh, I'm the future of this world, assuming we don't all kill each other. As for now, I'm going to spend the next two days in my hotel room streaming whatever, making sure that the staff will be able to confirm that I never left the hotel, while you're out here committing whatever misdemeanors and out right crimes, doing what you do. I wouldn't be surprised to see a pack of patrollers snatch your ass up and drag you all the way back to Mississippi."

"Bruh, that took a dark turn. We need to work on your humor skills."

Two Days Later... The Zealot and the Heretic met up again at the snowmobile rental facility.

The Zealot asked, "So...?"

The Heretics says nothing, but offered a smile which evolved into an ear to ear grin. The pair rode out to the site in silence, radio and otherwise. That is, until they reached their destination. Seeing the large hole in the ice and repelling equipment all set up, the Zealot could only say, "What the…?"

"Yeah, right! Pretty freaking awesome huh? We used these special mobile drills back North Dakota for fracking, before I realized how bad that whole thing was. But the beauty of them, is that you can drill on an angle. So, based on our calculations, I drilled at a forty-five-degree slope, for just over a hundred yards."

"And where did you get the equipment to…"

"I borrowed it overnight, and took it back before they missed it."

"How did you last so long in the service?"

"Same as you."

"Really?"

"Well, I adapt, whereas you conform."

The Zealot gave his friend a grimace.

"But you're burying the lead here. So, I ran one of those fiber optic lines that we used in the field to do inspections down there. Take a look at the pics I got."

"What the hell…?" the Zealot exclaimed.

But before the Heretic could elaborate, the pair heard the low rumble of snowmobiles headed towards them.

The Heretic called out, "What the hell…?"

A couple of minutes later, five snowmobiles, carrying seven passengers stopped right in front of the hole in the ice. Upon dismounting her snowmobile their leader gasped, "What the hell…?" Stepping over to the hole, she stared in. "My name is Meriwa and I represent the elders of our tribe. But more importantly, for you, do you have a permit for whatever it is that you're doing here?"

It was clear to both the Zealot and Heretic, that their new guest knew enough about oil drilling to know that they weren't doing that.

The Zealot began to speak, "I'm sorry ma'am, but I can't tell..."

The Heretic interrupted his friend, "Yes, we can't tell you how sorry we are. We were doing a bit of research for the university. But we'll pack up and leave right away."

While the Zealot grimaced, he remained silent, allowing his teammate to play things out, for the moment.

Although much of her face was covered, Meriwa's inaudible response took the Heretic back to his youth and the response of many a sister leveled towards him back in the day in Gulfport, Mississippi.

"Oil drilling is to the south, and the university is that way. But you guys rode in from the west, straight from town. So, what's down there?" Meriwa asked.

The Zealot gave the Heretic a side look, as he bluffed his way through, "We're just doing some geological research stuff. We're the contractors they hired to take the samples. Whatever we gather, we'll be taking back to the eggheads, you know?"

Meriwa twisted her face a bit before replying, "And for that you're drilling at an angle?"

For a moment the Heretic was stumped, but the Zealot offered, "Sometimes you can get a more diverse sample, if you drill at an angle."

Meriwa, seemingly ignoring the Zealot's answer, offered a thought of her own, "You know that this patch of unassuming ice is a holy place to my tribe? Our oral tradition states that gods from the heavens visited my people here and brought them many gifts. Of course, who believes in such things? Right?"

The pair of outsiders stood silent not knowing quite how to respond.

Meriwa continued, "Tell you what, I'm gonna let the pair of you go with a warning. But get a permit the next time, or I'll have you both locked up." Meriwa's cohorts, several of them armed, looked on in puzzlement. Clearly, this was not the woman they'd come to know. And yet, each of them followed her lead, as she mounted her snowmobile and rode out.

The Zealot and the Heretic stood in silence befuddled at what had just transpired, but minutes later they were securing their harnesses, the kind used in repelling. The hole wasn't wide enough for both of them to descend together, so the Heretic jumped in first, followed by the Zealot (who also unreeled a third, back up line should their two lines become disabled somehow).

The images he and the Zealot had taken two days before had indicated that there was a gap between where the ice ended and the ship began. Essentially, the alien craft sat in an ice cavern. Once he descended, the Heretic dangled just beyond the end of his ice tunnel, above the craft as he checked his Geiger counter, but it didn't read anything significant. And his digital spectrometer didn't pick up any known toxic gases. Removing his mask, the Heretic took a deep breath and smiled, as he gave his comrade's line a strong tug. Calling out over his headset, he teased the Zealot, "Dude, please try not to pee or shit yourself on the way down. I would really take offense were that to happen." The Heretic knew quite well, that wouldn't happen. On the contrary, despite the fact that he doubted the Zealot's reasoning on many things, he never questioned his courage.

"I heard you like it like that."

"Dude, that's so passé. The new thing is ASRM."

"What's that?"

"It's sounds."

"Sounds like what?"

"Never mind, just get down here. We need to be out of here before dark, and your girlfriend slowed us down already."

Within minutes, the Zealot had descended the hundred-yard ice slide. "Yo Bro, let's go!"

He didn't have to ask twice. As the Heretic uncoupled his line clamp, and quickly descended to the cavern floor, calling out all along the way. "Wow, wow, wow…"

Once they reached the floor the Zealot replied, "For once I agree with you, wow indeed!" The ship was various shades of purple, oscillating between being closer to red and then to blue, but the pair was unsure if it was the ship shifting colors, or was it simply their perspective shifting as even the slightest movement seemed to impact where they saw the vessel's hull along the color spectrum.

The ship itself had to be over a hundred yards long and its glow illuminated the cavern enough for the pair of explorers to remove and store away their helmet mounted halogen lights.

The Heretic turned to his right to see in the darkness two Sphinx looking creatures sitting side by side, their tales lightly buried in ice. "Wow…!!!"

"Wow ain't enough…" The Zealot answered, clearly astonished.

At the sight, the pair stood frozen like the monuments, before the mythical creatures, prior to turning back to the vessel. Stepping over, the Heretic reached out his hand and touched the vessel, and as he did, the Zealot called out, "Dude!"

But as he touched the ship, the Heretic tilted his head and replied, "Dude?"

The Zealot then placed his hand on the star craft as well, "Dude..."

The craft was slightly warm to the touch. The Zealot offered, "Hmm, I'm guessing this thing is fusion powered and that it's in some sort of sleep mode. And its shell is just warm enough to melt away the surrounding ice."

"And...?" the Heretic tilted his head towards his comrade.

"Yes, I feel it too."

"We're not interfacing with it, it's interfacing with us." The Heretic paused for a moment, seemingly lost in thought. "It's like it has an adaptive interface, capable of communicating with any sentient being."

The Zealot removed his hand for a moment, "I think it's doing a data dump from each of us, replicating every bit of information our brains hold."

"And maybe even our consciousness..." the Heretic added.

After careful consideration, the Zealot placed his hand back on the craft, "But I don't sense that it has bad intent."

"Me neither. Let's see if we can find a way in."

"You would say that."

"Hey, I know how this works out in Sci-Fi movies. Curiosity is always the fatal flaw. But this is real life. What if Columbus, had never reached out into the unknown?"

The Zealot gave his friend a death stare.

"Okay, he failed his way into the history books."

"He had a good publicist and the right complexion for the adulation."

"Alright then, my very woke, light, bright and damn near white brother."

"Still, I'm not down with going inside. Think about if the situation were reversed? If we were to visit another world, we'd be sure not to contaminate the world we're visiting, but we'd still keep things in our ship the way we need them to be for our survival."

"Ah, I get you. The oxygen we breathe today was toxic to living creatures eight hundred million years ago."

"And it's very reactive. To someone from another planet our atmosphere could very well be like walking in acid."

"…and the conditions inside the ship might be very toxic to us human, no spacesuit wearing brothers. Gotcha. Okay, so let's recon the fool out of this place before we go."

As the two walked around the craft snapping pictures, they conversed further.

The Heretic, not being able to let go of something he sensed above, "Did something about the woman up top strike you funny?"

"Honestly, yes."

The two of them came to the same realization, in the same moment. They both rushed back to their descent cords. Giving each one a hard pull, each gave way. "She knew what was down here!" the Heretic shouted.

"Yes, she did." The Zealot replied as he had already moved on from their literal lifelines. His eyes danced around the dimly lit cavern searching for opportunities he could leverage into a means of escape.

The Heretic, still shook by Meriwa's betrayal, sighed heavily and cursed as he too scanned the area for alternative means of escape.

"Dude, you got to let it go and move on. If we have any chance whatsoever of escaping this place, we both have to be totally locked in!"

"You're right, bruh." The Heretic turned to face the ship. "You know what? Since it seems that this thing can read minds, why don't we see if it has any ideas?"

The Zealot froze in his tracks, then turned to face the spaceship as well. "Hmm..."

The pair of contractors again walked towards the craft, then placing their hands on it again, felt the other worldly AI enter their minds once more. Seconds later, the cavern was filled with light, as the ship awoke. Then a searing white-hot beam of light exploded from the front of the craft, and into the forward wall of the cavern, cutting a ship sized hole through the glacier ice.

"Damn!" exclaimed the Heretic.

"Damn straight!" answered the Zealot, as he tightened his chin straps. "How do you say it in Mississippi? It's time to git... And I don't know if it matters, but it would be nice to be able to confirm the exact direction that tunnel will take us."

"Bruh, I got you." Knowing that their GPS devices would not work that far below the surface, the Heretic pulled out his compass. "Analogue, baby...!"

"But you still don't know where that takes us, do you?"

"No, but I know that you memorized all the mapping for this mission, as you always do. Right?"

"You know I did, it's called mission prep. But what if I had fallen and bumped my head or something?"

"I'd have to trust the Universe on that one."

Gathering himself, the Zealot explained, "No complaints here, but this path is going to lead us out into the bay. We'll have to jump in and swim for land."

"Or maybe we'll be able to get enough of a signal to place a call?"

"Dude. Look, we'll just have to see when we get there, but be prepared to swim. Worst case, I'll swim to shore and come back for you. But let's get to stepping, because as this ice refreezes, it's going to get slick and make the miles we've got to go all the harder."

After glancing back at the alien craft and snapping on their helmet lanterns, the pair departed the cavern, and entered the darkening tunnel of slushy ice, not knowing fully what to expect.

About two miles into their trek both of them noticed something reflecting back through the darkness at them. As they closed in on the source of the reflection, frozen within the ice, the Heretic shook his head in the disbelief, "What the hell? Dude, doesn't that look like a life vest?"

"Kind of, but it couldn't be. I mean that makes no sense."

After giving one another a quick glance they each removed their ice picks and began digging into the side of the tunnel.

In a rare show of emotion, the Zealot cried out, "Look, it's a life vest, and there's a second one beside it!" As they dug with their ice picks, they found two wetsuits and a self-inflating raft. Then he commented in disbelief as he loaded up on a sundry of spoils. "This makes absolutely no sense."

"Unless…"

"Unless what?"

"What if this is the Alchemist's doing?"

"What?"

"What if he or she, put these things here, knowing that one day, we'd need them?"

"And who are we, that anyone would do that?"

As the Heretic completed putting on his newfound wetsuit, he answered, "Good point. But if we are to believe the evidence right in front of us, regardless of how unbelievable it may seem, the Alchemist not only knew the future, but also had agency enough to inject themselves into our timeline for their own purpose."

As the pair pushed forward towards the sea, the Zealot, after giving the matter serious thought, spoke again, "But why do it this way?"

"Explain…"

"I'm sure there were a thousand different points in which the Alchemist could have put their thumb upon the scale. So, why like this? I mean, why not stop old girl from cutting our lines? But instead our benefactor chooses to simply make our journey easier."

"So, you're saying that these items, won't actually change the outcome substantively?"

"Right."

"So maybe that's the point. This Alchemist has some sort of constraint, whereby substantively changing future outcomes is disallowed."

"Like a prime directive." The Zealot chimed in homage to an old television show.

"But apparently, they can provide comfort. If true, it's an appreciated, but slippery slope, if you ask me."

The Zealot added, "Or maybe, they just want us to know that there is someone or something watching over us from the rafters."

"You sound like…"

The Zealot cut his friend off, "Yeah, I've been around you for far too long."

"Hmm, I get that a lot."

"No doubt."

"Really, Bruh?"

Reaching the end of the ice tunnel, they inflated the raft, tethered it, and tossed it into the cold waters below. As they repelled the short distance to the bay below, a powerful blue light lit up the tunnel above them and shown out over the bay and into the waiting sky beyond. Moments later the light show ceased and the hole in the ice was no more.

After a good bit of rowing the pair reached the pier, and climbed up, leaving the dingy tied up below. The Heretic got down on his knees and kissed the ground, while the Zealot offered up a quick prayer of thanks.

"Everything is Written." the Zealot spoke into the vapors.

"Amen, brother. On this one thing we agree. Even the intervention of our benefactor."

Though they'd originally planned to hang out their final night in the land of northern lights, each knew that they'd do well to simply make it back to their hotel, and to the airport the following morning. But along the way they spotted a familiar face. It was Meriwa standing outside with her crew, enjoying the evening on the back patio of a local bar called *Dante's*. The Zealot and the Heretic couldn't help but step over to where the seven of them laughed and carried on. That is, until they heard the Heretic call out, "Meriwa!"

The laughing dark haired woman turned around, and stared down below, as her crew, one by one turned to see what had caught their leader's attention. Meriwa called out, "I'm surprised, but not totally. My spirit told me that you might be the real deal. But regardless, you were on holy land where our old gods are buried. And like so many others you were there to desecrate and ravage. When you do that, you get what you get."

One of the guys in Meriwa's crew slung a mug of brew at the Zealot before lunging at him from the deck. The others followed suit. It was two against seven, with six of those seven being Meriwa's security team. It was an unfair fight, which lasted less than ninety seconds. When it ended, only Meriwa was left standing from her crew, as she faced the Zealot and Heretic. As Meriwa's team lay in the snow, each with at least one broken bone, the Heretic separated Meriwa from her six-inch blade and slung it into one of the deck posts, causing her to fall to the ground in the process. Then he lifted Meriwa from the snow and held her up, as the Zealot stepped over and spoke to her in her native tongue,

"Sister, my grandmother was Inuit and I know that you have strayed from the path." Then switching back to English, as the Heretic released Meriwa back into the snow, the Zealot added loud enough for all to hear, "If you come at us, or anyone in our crew ever again, well, then you too, will get what you get." Not waiting for a reply from any of their fallen foes, the Zealot turned and walked away. He did this knowing full well, that there was a time when he and his compadre would have smoked these *fools* for their transgression. But they too, were on a different path.

The Heretic, a little slower in releasing the moment, allowed his gaze to linger on their fallen foes and the other locals, before also turning and heading off into the falling snow. And yet two steps later he called back over his shoulder, "You know proportional punishment is kind of a thing these days. You might want to look into it. Otherwise, you get what... well you know."

Next: *Long Walk to Never* (aka *Whatever, man...– Marketing Girl*)

Long Walk to Never (Living in the Moment)

Hi this is Marketing Girl. Believe it or not, Blerd finally let me pen one of these journals. Trust and believe, a girl has to call on the ancestors to pry his brown fingers from the keyboard. But at last, I'm here.

Okay, full disclosure. The only reason Blerd lets me write this one, is because he isn't here. It's just me and the girls. Cousin Kisha, the mute Nia, that heifer Voodoo Priestess and the Russian, Grime's girl (yeah right, how does Grimes have a girl, let alone, someone like her, but I digress). The mission de jour is to catch a thief. The Russian has intel that our thief is across the pond setting up meetings to shop his stolen booty.

But since we we're changing planes at JFK anyway, the ladies and I decide fly up early, so that we can spend the day shopping in New York, before our evening flight.

Upon landing, four of us connect at LGA and Uber down to Brooklyn to connect with The Russian at the Dekalb Market. It's mid-morning, so we're able to grab our own table, to discuss our business in private. But before we begin discussing the target, Kisha gives me a look, which clearly questions my choice in attire. While, they're all dressed for the long flight to come, I have on a sundress. Silly rabbit, doesn't she know that every girl has a fall back option when she can't decide. Mine, is my sundress. Big whoopee doo.

While the other ladies are talking about the thief, the art house that he's in league with, and the "blatant trafficking in pain" they're a part of, I'm checking my phone and wondering why my boy hasn't hit me up yet. I know he's in the Caribbean with the fellas, but he could send a text. If he's thinking about me, he would. But it's cool, because that heifer Voodoo Priestess is here with me, rather than back in

Jamaica. Oh, don't get me wrong. I *love* Voodoo Priestess. I really do. But she's a little too *free loving* to have around my man, if you know what I mean.

I hear the ladies mention "The Long Walk" one of my favorite paintings, which is one of the works stolen, my attention turns back to them. Well, that and the fact that Kisha calls out, "Hey, A D D, over here!" Kisha continues blabbing regarding details that I could not care less about. But it seems to make her feel good to do so, so I don't interrupt.

Oh, let me back up a minute and level set things. My main role in this little collective of ours, is that of an administrator. I field the requests, forward the actionable ones to Blerd, and coordinate the talent for each mission, Mission Impossible style. But in this particular case, I'm out in the field, because I have a talent for languages. Actually, I speak six languages fluently, from French to Mandarin, and in a pinch, I can get by in several others. What can I say, other than "Black Girl Magic".

The way we roll on these *on the low* "trips" is that everyone wears a transmitter in their ear (takes a special appliance to place and remove them, safely), that allows me to hear audio around them, and allows them to hear me translate anything worth mentioning, back to them. Of course, The Russian has her own tech, that she likes to use, so as always, I acquiesce. She knows our encryption scheme, since she wrote it, so asking me if it's okay that she uses her own earpiece each time, is really just her playing nice. But hell, she's *dating* Grimes. Heaven bless9 her confused soul. #prooftheressomeoneforeveryone

As the four of them pull out their tablets and jabber on about timelines and sight lines at the venue, I'm thinking about timelines and sight lines on my wedding day. Not that anything is confirmed, but I know. Blerd is the one. I just know it.

So, we experience a historic afternoon of shopping in NYC and board our flight to London. I check my phone again once we land and still no texts from Blerd. But then just as we're taking off for

Prague, a smiley face pops up on my phone. It's from Blerd. I smile. He's in Canada with the Zealot and Heretic, ice fishing or something. Da Hell? Doesn't matter, he should be ring shopping.

Long story short, we get to Prague (our fake passports work like a charm), and head directly into the countryside. It's beautiful beyond words, but cold (which for just a moment has me questioning my wardrobe choices, but just a moment). Each of the ladies dons their thermal gear (it masks them from infrared imaging), paints their faces black in some non-hypogenic product (sad) and step from our van into the night. Snapping on my headset, I check in with each of my sisters. Each responds loud and clear. Each of them has a number, and I speak that number as a prefix before translating what I hear coming across each headset. I have a monitor which displays each of them and it lights up whoever is speaking, so that I know who I'm translating for. I must admit, it's all quite clever.

The girls split into two teams, leap frogging each other as they approach the target so that they can watch each other's back (watching your "six" I think they call it). Team "A" is the Russian & Voodoo Priestess. Team "B" is Cousin Kisha and Nia. And though Nia happens to be mute (well to human ears anyway), Kisha's ability to hear without hearing (she's an intuit of the highest level), allows her to understand ninety percent of what Nia's saying without her signing anything. The Russian and Nia are armed with sidearms, whereas Kisha has her side piece, crossbow, darts and other toys (her sniper's rifle is in the van with me). Voodoo Priestess doesn't a gun, but she carries all of her mystic things with her, wherever she goes, plus a switchblade strapped to her thigh. You won't catch her napping in that regard. Besides, she is the one who can move without moving.

From my position, via my binoculars, I can see through the ceiling to floor windows which line the back of the villa, as the growing number of figures march across my line of sight onto the main floor. I confirm to my team that the art tour of potential buyers through the basement gallery is over, and that most of them are likely back upstairs. So, I greenlight them to proceed towards the villa's rear from their position in the woods behind the estate. Thus, per our plan, the buyers and sellers will be in the auction upstairs, while we execute our plan down below.

The Russian's recon intelligence, is flawless as always, so the team finds no surprises during their sojourn through the darkness. Their gear hides their presence from any automated electronic monitoring, up until they reach the hedge lining the outdoor pool (a privacy fence of sorts) which sits in the rear of the villa on the basement level. The video feed I'm getting from them, even enhanced, is pretty much useless, so I focus in on their words, and the ambient sound around them. Our main impediments are the four armed guards positioned across two entry points.

The ladies are armed, but choose to first try a less violent means to gain entry. The ladies look to Nia, and she knows it's her turn now. With her back pressed into the hedge behind which they are hid, Nia speaks into the black forest. Her lips move in apparent silence, but in mere moments the most amazing thing transpires. A swarm of humming birds descend upon the four-man security team. Through the live feed I can see their confusion, swatting their hands around in chase of a seemingly invisible foe. Our feathered allies target their tender, exposed parts. As the moment builds, one the four pulls out his side arm and frantically fires off a shot, missing the winged ghosts in the darkness, and hitting one of his associates in the leg. Yelling and cussing ensues in their native tongue, and two of the men begin carrying the wounded one, up and around from the basement level and towards the front yard, while the trigger happy one follows profusely apologizing all along the way, even as the humming birds still give chase.

Once the men are out of sight, the ladies move in towards the abandoned doorways. While Kisha brought enough charges to blow off several doors, there is no need. The Russian explains, "Not only can I crack virtual locks, I crack them in real life too."

When the door opens, I hold my breath listening for an alarm. There is none, only the whine of an alert that a door has been opened, allowing the entrant time to disarm the system. The Russian scurries to the keypad and enters the code to silence the would be tattle tale. As the ladies turn back towards the room, to take in the scene and the expected cache of stolen works of art, they are assailed with the unexpected.

Not only do they see the stolen art mounted along the basement walls, next to each piece is a human being chained to the wall beside their work. This is not just an auction of art, but of the creators of that art as well. I hear The Russian cry out as she falls to her knees, next to one bound down artist, weeping as she pulls at the woman's chains. Voodoo Priestess is as still and silent a as stone statue, with only her scanning eyes revealing any hint that she is among the living. Kisha is barking instructions to her team. She realizes that they'll need to get these captives out of this hellhole. And that means a fight. She says these things as though someone is listening, but her words are just as much for herself as anyone (in this one regard, Kisha is just like her cousin, Blerd, always trying to speak order into chaos). But Nia, the human trafficking survivor, reverts back to that once imprisoned little girl, as she's curls up in a corner. I gasp realizing what I'm seeing and begin screaming "No, no, no...!" into their headsets.

Kisha looks towards The Russian, but before she can even open her mouth, The Russian is using her bolt cutter on the chains of the first artist.

Kisha realizes without infrared proof suits for each of the captives, the Villa's alarms will cry out like a demon from hell once they step into the back lawn. Kisha leans down and hugs Nia, "Come on darling." And once Nia is on her feet, Kisha asks the young woman, "I know I'm asking a lot, but we're going to need some cover getting out of here."

And though Kisha doesn't provide any specifics, Nia knows exactly what she's asking. Nia turns towards the wall which lines the rear of the basement, and speaks through the walls, into the forest beyond. Her lips move, and she speaks with a grace hidden to the human ear.

There are ten artists being held captive, and The Russian, through her tears, cuts each one free of their metal chains. When the last one is free, they gather everyone and proceed as quietly as possible through the basement's, latter-day, door of no return.

Realizing that we'll need to load all of these artists into our SUV, I break cover and head down an unpaved road closer to their position. "I'm heading to extraction point B." I call out over their headsets. This is always the plan, should there be an injury.

Hearing them gathering the victims, I depart my position. I hear the alarm go off, as they enter the backyard, with the formerly enslaved artists. I glance down into my partitioned monitor trying to find some glimpse of order in the streams from their headcams, but all I see is chaos and the eerie sight of random forest animals scurrying past them towards the house. Given that my team is marching towards the pitch black forest, I shouldn't expect to see much of anything. But now I'm hearing popping sounds as my teammates turn back towards the villa to return fire. The security team turns on all the property's rear facing flood lights, making it near impossible Kisha and The Russian to hit their targets as they attempt to provide cover for one another.

Not seeing how they could possibly make it to my position unscathed, I decide to take the large SUV off-road and make a bee line to their position.

The fire fight escalates while our team works back towards me, as the hostages scramble into the SUV. Kisha tosses her gun, which I assume means that she's out of bullets. I instruct our guests to get as low as possible in the vehicle, while I remain upright watching out for my crew. Voodoo Priestess senses a pair of security guards attempting to flank us and taps the Russian on the shoulder, who shoots the first one dead, but the second one reaches her before she can put a bullet in him. She slaps his gun hand and then attempts to sweep his feet out beneath him, but he's too heavy for that to work. The pair wrestle for his gun, until suddenly and silently, an arrow appears in the man's neck from the bow of Kisha. His life spurts out with each heartbeat.

Now that all of the artists are crammed into the vehicle, there's no reason to continue to engage the enemy, so the ladies high tail it back to me. They jump on the running boards on each side of our ride and I throw us into reverse, hoping to spin us around when I can find a gap in the trees.

Suddenly, there's this blinding light and I'm sitting in the front passenger seat, the windshield is shattered, Voodoo Priestess is driving, and my girls and all of the artists are cheering and crying hysterically. Kisha is hugging and kissing me as best she can from the seat behind me. The Russian is calling out over and over "Ty Zhiv!!!" which translates into "You're Alive!!!"

I notice that Voodoo Priestess has blood running from her nose, and her eyes are severely bloodshot. She's laughing and crying at the same time, as we're driving away. She motions for me to lean in towards her. I do so and she says, as our guests are calling out praises to the Higher Being in their native tongues, "Marketing Girl, you know how I can kind of freeze time and move around a bit while it's frozen? Well, truth is, I can do slightly more than that. To a very small degree, I can actually move back in time."

Feeling newly displaced, I interrupt her, "What's going on here?"

Voodoo Priestess pauses, then continues, "As you were backing us out of there, a bullet came through the front windshield, and struck you in the head. We all freaked out for a moment, but I knew that I could do something. So, I made the choice. I went back five seconds or so in time, and pulled you out of harm's way. And now you're alive."

"Whoa..." I'm speechless beyond that.

"Yeah, I know that's a lot to process, and the effort nearly killed me. Each time I do this it gets worse. So yes, I can move back through time, but it comes at a price. Also, there can be side effects from what

I did to you. It can alter your perception of time. It might be a temporary or it could be permanent. At times you may have the sense that everything is happening at once, conversely there may be times, when an hour feels like a week. How that will play out for you, only time will tell, literally. But know that with these things, there are always consequences. The universe is resolved in this.

Next: *Don't You Worry 'bout a Thing.* (*Liars and the Women Who Believe Them – Marketing Girl*)

Don't You Worry 'Bout A Thing.

"**W**ake up asshole. I want you awake when this goes down."

Through my doubled vision, I couldn't really make out my agitator's face, not enough to clearly know who it was.

Standing right in front of me, my tormentor yelled over his shoulder, "Give him another shot of the juice. He needs to know who this is and what this is!"

I felt a dull sense of pressure in my right shoulder, but nothing else. Then, just moments later, I felt my consciousness fully engaged once again. Seeing clearly then, an expression of recognition must have swept over my face.

"That's right, asshole, it's me!"

I guess, I should back up a bit. After the murder of Money, I and my core team relocated from Atlanta, since we couldn't help but assume that our eternal foe, Entropy, who orchestrated Money's death, was close on our tails. We traded some favors for new SSNs and passports, and hit the road.

However, word reached us that one of our favorite high school teachers, Mrs. Lamont, had gone missing, apparently kidnapped. Actually, she was my homeroom teacher from eighth to twelfth grade. She held a special place in my heart. One day, during our eleventh-grade year, she essentially told the girls in our homeroom class that they were sleeping on me, and that one day I'd make a wonderful husband. Being older now, I see how such things are so clearly apparent once you've lived a little. But having the thought and then expressing it to our class was, and still is, an amazing thing to me. But the most important thing she did, was to consistently share life lessons, particularly with the young ladies who came through her class, she was always trying to pour knowledge into them. We knew she actually cared.

So, when we heard the news that she was missing, Marketing Girl and I caught a flight to Atlanta the same day. I'd not seen or spoken to Mrs. Lamont in at least ten years and yet it was never a question that I'd join the effort to find her.

When Marketing Girl and I landed, we headed straight to the meet up spot on the northside of town. Using an online alias, I booked a dining room there for us. It was an Italian restaurant which I knew had a private room. I'd sent word to everyone in our core group. When we arrived, Marketing Girl and I headed straight to the back room. Pulling back the black curtain, we took in the twelve-person table in front of us. Left to right, I saw the Zealot, the Heretic, Cousin Kisha, Grimes, his *girlfriend* The Russian (they happened to have an open relationship) and recent college graduate, Nia. The only two missing from our core group, were Voodoo Priestess and our local OG from the hood, Roughneck.

I smiled and offered to them all, "Thanks for coming on such short notice. Here's the…"

But before I could finish my sentence, Marketing Girl interrupted, "Where is Ms. Thing?" Ms. Thing, was just one of Marketing Girls' names for Voodoo Priestess.

The Russian offered, "Grimes and I both reached out. She said that she'd be here, but didn't give an ETA." The Russian and Voodoo Priestess had become pretty tight since the US born Jamaican had done a reading for the silver hair Russian expat (Voodoo had the Russian cast three stones upon the waters of an island lake, years ago, from which she read her future).

Grimes laughed at his girlfriend's answer, "And y'all know what that means. Island time, all day long!"

Grimes and The Russian were admittedly an odd pair. But Grimes had a type (don't we all), or should I say two types, Eastern European women and homeless women. The Eastern European thing was his business, but, in my mind at least, the homeless thing, seemed to be power thing with him. I stepped to him several times on the subject, but he was as thick as dried out peanut butter on the matter. For her part The Russian was a flavor of sapiosexual, and Grimes as a hacker was top notch. In fact, he had a lot of cred in those digital highways. Conversely, I kept my doings on the low.

"What about Roughneck?" I asked, now that we'd gone there.

Kisha gave me that look. "What you think?" She said in regard to her sometime paramour. Roughneck was our local muscle when we had the need. He attended our high school, but graduated before either Kisha or I got there. But everybody in the hood knew exactly who Roughneck was. Plus, he'd done a couple of extended bids upstate.

And while I try to stay out of grown folks' business, Cousin Kisha would come to me regarding Roughneck more so to vent than to ask for any advice I might have. She'd lament, "He's just not what I had in mind for my life. Ex-felon, Ex-wife, two baby mommas and counting, plus he didn't even have a bank account until I made him get one last year. And on top of all of that, he's old." He never shared his age, but since he graduated ten years before we did, he was at least ten years older than us. But if he'd ever been held back in school, which was certainly a reasonable possibility, he could have been even older.

"But..." I'd say to Kisha, "he's in extremely good shape. I mean, I'm fit, in a triathlete sort of way. But that dude is chiseled." I always try to be supportive.

Then she'd say some variation of "All true. But you know how many women I've called dummies for dating guys like him?" and then we'd move on. The pathology was always the same.

This time all I needed to do was give her a nod acknowledging her angst. "Alright then. As always, we keep it moving. We got to hit all the spots in South Dekalb, and a few in Decatur. Russian, I think that on this particular search effort, you may need stay off the field and run communications." Acknowledging how her blonde hair and very white skin, even in that time, might draw undue attention (Whites folks freely roaming black communities was no longer a thing, but white folks going around asking questions, especially with Russian accents, was an entirely different thing). I added, "But I definitely want you front and center for the phase two."

I carried on sharing the plan with the others (though as usual, Grimes was on his phone and not listening to a word I said), and all the while I was glancing over towards my cousin looking for her to shake the funk, and reengage. Despite all we strive to be, there are times when our emotions make fools of us all, and maybe that's okay, ...in small doses anyway.

As we prepared to break camp I wanted to say one last thing, "I just want y'all to know…"

But the Zealot interrupted me, "Blerd, I think I speak on behalf of everyone here, that it's an honor to be able to return just some of the kindness you've shown to others over the years. Don't worry about it."

Everyone at the table nodded in agreement. I'm not an emotional guy, but that touched me.

Done with whatever he was doing on his phone, Grimes, who we deemed Lord of the Underworld for his mastery of the dark web, spoke, "All of this love is well and good, but what are we going to do? Are we going door to door looking for Mrs. Lamont? What's the deal?"

I smirked a bit, "Don't you worry, I have a plan. I got this…"

****

…okay, so now you're caught up.

I had devised this plan on the flight to Atlanta. At the time, it seemed like a brilliant idea to use myself as bait. Mrs. Lamont was beloved in our community, so I reasoned that this might just be an attempt by Entropy to lure me and my crew back to Atlanta. Thus, I figured that if I roamed around the hood, Candler Road, Glenwood Drive and Flat Shoals, that word would get back to ol' boy, aka the kidnapper. I was reasonably sure that they'd take me to him, rather than smoke me on the spot. Well, at least I got that last part right.

Finally, able to pry my swollen eyes open, I squinted through the all too bright lights to see my accuser. It was Koshi, the drug dealer whose trap house we'd burned down many years before. He was flanked in the all so sparse garage by two of his street soldiers. "Still in the game, huh? Long time, no see." I remarked through the pain of lacerations and bruising inflicted upon my face and body.

"My business partners suggested that I put some time between your crime against me and your inevitable punishment."

Seeing the lower case "e" tattooed on his neck, I amended his reply, "Strongly suggested, perhaps?"

"True, my partners have no concern for the finer details of street justice, but at the end of the day, you're here, so does it really matter?"

Pulling at my bonds, I answered, "Nope."

"Knowing some of the things you've done, it's clear that you're not afraid to die."

"No, I know that I've pissed off enough people, that dying in my sleep is probably not gonna happen for me. I've accepted it."

"I know the same. Too many bodies, too many enemies and too many *friends* looking to take my place." The college educated chemist lamented as he gave a side eye to his compadres.

"But no quick death for me, huh?"

"Nah, Bruh. Given what you've done, I can't do that."

In that moment, I noted the plastic sheeting beneath my chair. "I see. So, now that you have me, what are you going to do with Mrs. Lamont? Can I assume that you'll let her go?"

"I was going to, but I think not now. I need to send a message to the community. And while I know who you are, as do my partners, no one else really remembers you. Hell, until you burned down our spot, most of my crew didn't know who the hell you were. And if they did, you were just some nerd who attended their high school years ago. But everybody knows Mrs. Lamont."

"Koshi, if I may...?"

"Proceed."

"I know it won't change my situation, which I'm fine with. But you're not from around here, so you really don't understand who this woman is to this community. I think you'd be making a huge mistake in hurting her any more than you already have."

I noticed that the two young men guarding me, glanced towards Koshi pensively waiting on his next words. "I know she means a lot around here, but this chrome on our waist means a whole lot more."

In that moment I saw it for the first time, Koshi was clearly smelling himself. Before then, I'd respected how Koshi ran his game. Never seeking the "respect" that so many the young men in his employment got caught up in. Instead he'd run things from the shadows, in ice cold fashion. Say what you will about the harm he brought to the community; you could not argue that he wasn't smart about his hustle. But I could see, at long last, he'd succumbed to the prideful-ness that absolute power brings. Having seen several of Koshi's soldiers in and out of the room next to where I was being held, I commented shrugging my shoulders, "So, y'all just gonna keep her in the kitchen?"

"Yeah, and so what?" Koshi had taken the bait.

"So, when y'all get tired of punching me and really get down to business, it's going to get noisy, she's gonna hear it, and it's gonna freak her out. I don't think y'all want to be dealing with that, assuming that y'all plan to be quick and neat with her when the time comes? So, maybe move her to the living room."

Koshi wasn't so far gone as to not understand that having a hysterical woman screaming in his kitchen would not be cool. Koshi nodded to his lieutenant, and the lieutenant motioned for the soldier standing by the door to the kitchen to proceed in moving Mrs. Lamont to the front living room.

I nodded to the two remaining men, and said to Koshi, "Good. Let's get on with it."

What I said was true, but neither of them realized my ulterior motive. No, I didn't want Mrs. Lamont to hear me being tortured. But more importantly, I wanted my crew to hear through the microphone hidden in my clothing, exactly where Mrs. Lamont was, or would be in the building. The garage was in the back of the building, and the living room was in the front. This would make her rescue a little easier for my team. Plus, if gunfire should arise when they came for me, she'd be on the other side of the house. But my "Let's get on with it." was also a coded message for my team, that they could come and get me now.

However, things outside were not progressing exactly as planned. My team had indeed surrounded the trap house. While Kisha was in the rear rooftop sniper position and effectively had command of the battlefield since she had the best vantage point. The Zealot and the Heretic were in the forward sniper positions. Although Kisha was almost as good a shot as the Zealot and certainly better than Heretic at long distances, the fellas were better than any of the rest of us in hand to hand combat, into which this situation could very well devolve. Nia, the mute, sat way back, in the yard of an abandoned house down the street, with a pack of stray dogs sitting around her. At her command, they'd charge the house, if needed. The Russian and Grimes were in a parked rental van on the street that ran along the back of the property. They were our logistical hub through which our private channel ran. But The Russian was very nice when it came to gunplay and decent with her hands too. And though she was in her early forties by this point in our lives, she was still a head turner. Fixing her face before she exited the van, she knew that her looks could get her close enough to inflict real damage. As The Russian, headed down the dark street from the van to the rear of property, Grimes spoke over our private line, "The fox is loose. ETA to her mark, twenty seconds." The plan was for the forward team to assault the front of the house, being sure not shoot on any line in which a bullet could enter the living room, while The Russian came around back to the garage to free me or to flank our opponents should this be an extended gunfight.

But about five seconds before the assault was to begin and as Koshi threw a combination into my midsection knocking me and the chair to which I was tied over (he wanted to get in a couple more licks before things got *messy*), a background voice came over everyone's Bluetooth earpiece, "What the hell are y'all doing?" The voice was Roughneck's.

"Roughneck?" Kisha knew the voice, but still she was startled to hear him.

"Yeah, baby girl, it's me." Having grabbed the Heretic's headset, he answered Kisha. Roughneck continued, "I saw y'all posted up around as I came up. Y'all gonna get a lot of folks killed doing this, this way. Let me handle this. All Koshi's boys know me, and they know better than fool with me." Roughneck tossed the headset back to the Heretic and strolled into Koshi's yard. The soldiers realizing who it was, understood that this was a king to king thing, and there was no beef between the two, so they let him pass uncontested. Of course, Roughneck had a piece stuck beneath his belt in his back, but everybody there was strapped too.

Going through the front door, he took one look at Mrs. Lamont, and announced to everyone in the room, "Really? Why do y'all have her tied up? Where she gonna go?" pointing out the obvious, that she was an old lady in a room full of armed men.

Then he spoke to one of the Koshi's men standing there, "Where is he?"

The worker bee pointed through the kitchen towards the garage door. Roughneck walked briskly through the kitchen and burst into the garage. There he saw Koshi doing some sort of Mohammed Ali foot shuffle dance over me as I laid there on the floor with a fresh nose bleed. In three quick steps Roughneck closed the distance between him and Khosi, delivering a hard-right hand across Kohsi's chin, knocking the *Tiger of East Atlanta*, as the kingpin sometimes referred to himself, smooth out.

Roughneck knelt down to untie me and helped me to my feet. As we headed back towards the kitchen, he asked the lieutenant and a couple others who'd entered the garage, "Were y'all really gonna let him smoke Mrs. Lamont?"

"Nah, Bruh. He just said he was gonna use her as bait to bring that nerd back to town, the one that torched the old shack. But Koshi switched up on us!"

Roughneck came to a complete stop in the Livingroom and tilted his head in confusion. "This is Mrs. Lamont! Look out that window. See that school? Not only did she teach most of you, for some of you *youngins*, she taught your mama and your daddy too. This woman had seniority, she could have transferred to any school in the district, but she didn't. Her husband made good money, they could have moved to Dunwoody, but they *chose* to stay. If your folks cussed you out and you couldn't go home, who did you call to come get you?"

"Mrs. Lamont." The lieutenant confessed.

"That's right, so what the hell are y'all doing?" Entering the living room and fighting back even the hint of being overwhelmed with emotion, Roughneck shook his head as he removed the blindfold and gag from Mrs. Lamont's mouth, "Y'all know y'all ain't shit..."

Once Roughneck removed her bounds, Mrs. Lamont leaned forward, placing her face in her hands, and wept bitterly.

The lieutenant pulling the bandana from around his face, conceded. "No, we ain't shit." Tossing the rag to the floor, he announced, "I'm done y'all. Tell Koshi, whatever when he wakes up. I don't care. I didn't sign up for this." Then knelling down beside Mrs. Lamont, the lieutenant wrapped his arm around the her. "Let me drive you home." He said this knowing that doing this would very likely mean that he'd be arrested and spend years in a cell.

But even as he did this, Mrs. Lamont, though she had not a mark on her beyond her bruised wrists, cried, "Oh, y'all hurt me so bad, I just want to die..." Having her kids do this to her, had taken the old woman's will to live. One of the other soldiers in the room slid down one of the side walls staring into nothing, as his former teacher wept bitter tears. Then a second, third and fourth soldier descended to the floor where they stood. Each of them sat unmoving adrift in their collective shame.

Roughneck, knowing that the lieutenant would at this point honor his word, turned and walked out the door into the front yard. I limped along behind him, pinching my bloody nose. The first to greet us in the street were the Heretic and the Zealot as they arose from their hiding places and marched towards us hosting wide grins. Next, Grimes and The Russian drove up. Grimes laughed, "You know that was some stupid shit you did, right?"

I shrugged, giving him an indifferent non-answer, all the while still holding my nose as I used my free hand to remove the tiny speaker stuck deep into my ear.

Then through the darkness, I saw Kisha, flanked by Nia, stroll up. I knew well the look on Kisha's face. It was the look of a woman fully in love with her man. Kisha offered a faux grimace, "So, where you been?"

"You know *where I been*..." Roughneck had missed a couple of payments to the state, and as most caught up in our judicial system can testify to, when you're free, most often you're not really *free*.

"How'd you get out?" Kisha asked as she approached Roughneck

"My wife bailed me out."

"You mean your ex-wife, right?"

Roughneck stared down into the ground.

Signifying, Grimes let out a "Oh, oh..."

Kisha shook her head in disbelief, "Do you mean that all this time...???" She took a step back before she yelled, "You're still married?" Pausing for another moment, she added "I'm such a fool..."

Roughneck lifted his face to Kisha, "Well, as far as we're concerned, we're divorced, we just never filed the paper work."

Putting the pieces together, Kisha filled in the blanks, "Her name is still on your bank account, that's how and why she bailed you out. No, actually, it's her bank account, right?"

"Yeah, back in the day, it helped keep what I did on the low, and it's still *helpful*... even if we're not living as man and wife."

Frustrated, Kisha turned and marched away in strong strides, with Roughneck following close behind her.

Grimes who by this time was standing next to me, said in astonishment, "Kisha is a human lie detector, how could she miss that?"

The Russian offered, "She is a woman first, and a woman always believes what she wants to believe, even Kisha."

While we all loved Roughneck, my gut had always told me, that their relationship would implode at some point. But then there was a part of me, a part that I kept suppressed, that reasoned that if he made her happy, then what difference did all of these mortal conventions mean? Growing up, Kisha's mother had an "understanding" with an older, married gentleman. He contributed to their bills each month, and stepped in when unexpected financial misfortune brewed up. Kisha detested the arrangement, and we both thought that her mother could do better. And hearing other family members degrade auntie, didn't help. Only my mother faithfully supported auntie through it all. The whole situation saddened Kisha and me as children.

...but as I've grown older, I've seen the truth of things, in that plenty of folks, particularly older ones, often live within these *understandings & arrangements*, for various reasons, and injecting the black and white morality of a child, into a full-grown adult situation can be ill fitting.

...and yet, I did not suggest to Kisha at any time, that she should lower her relationship expectations. Not because of some moral piety, but because I've known her basically all her life, and I knew that this was the one thing she didn't want.

Grimes, still flabbergasted by my *plan*, grabbed a hold of my neck and shoulders squeezing as he said, "Dude, you know if that bastard hadn't been a sadistic mo-fo, and had simply put a bullet in your head, we'd be planning your funeral right now."

"And we still may be." Announced The Russian as she looked up from the faint glow of her laptop. "Apparently Entropy had Koshi's new trap house under surveillance. They've got a strike team headed here now. Best guess, they'll be here in ten." This indeed was the real trap all along, now sprung. We realized that this was likely the game all along.

Grimes handed me my headset and I offered the team a simple choice. "What do y'all want to do? Run or fight?"

I waited for a moment, and one by one everyone said fight. Then covering my mic, I looked at The Russian, and softly said, "Are you sure?" I asked, because she was the only person there who had bigger price on her head than me. Not only did Entropy want her, several nations states did too. I, nor anyone else on the team, could say that. She was the most at risk among us. If she wanted to dip right then, we would have all understood.

The silver hair woman replied, "Absolutely."

The Zealot added, "Then I suggest that we pull back to those woods behind where Nia was posted up. I'm sure they'll have night googles too, but we know the terrain better than them, and we wouldn't be risking any civilians back in the cut."

The Heretic chimed in, "With a quickness people, we need to position and prep. Let's move!" Within our group, we had a flexible leadership model. I led on all things strategic, and even more so since Money was murdered (with his connections, he opened up avenues and access few others could). But in tactical matters, the Heretic and Zealot led. And so on and so forth, we each led in our own lanes. As a rule, we didn't have ego drama, as our work was larger than any one of us. On that note, we had Marketing Girl relocate our van to a nearby underpass, for her own safety.

After finding the tallest tree in that dark forest, I set upon climbing it. Though, I was trained in several martial arts, I had no illusions about my usefulness on the ground, against any of the armed professional mercenaries headed our way. So, I sought the highest point on the battle field from which I could safely and most effectively aid my teammates. If I had to swing these hands of mine, it would mean that things had truly gone to hell. Then my watch vibrated with the notice of an incoming message. Illuminating the message, I announced to the team through my headset, "Caribbean Gumbo, is on the ground and in transit." Which meant that Voodoo Priestess had landed and was ridesharing her way to meet up with us.

Then from my vantage point, I heard it; the distinctive sound of an approaching helicopter. It halted its approach at the street which boarded the north end of the woods in which we hid. I was able see two ropes fall from the craft, and black cloaked individuals sliding down into the darkness. "Eight bad guys, fully loaded approaching from the north."

Once they fell beneath the tree line, I lost direct sight of them, but as I was pulling out my infra-red enabled tablet to track their heat signatures, Kisha, the intuit, called out, "I see them cousin. They're looking for our trail. Ah, I think they found it. They're coming through the tree line now."

Being higher up, above the others, I couldn't really see details of any happenings on the ground, but I could see clearly the "field" and the players on it, as glowing dots. I could warn our team, when any of the hostiles got close to one of them.

Our intent in any confrontation was to never be the ones firing the first shot. So, we waited, until they reached the point, which we knew they would, where our footprints disappeared. One of them called out, "What the hell..."

We'd climbed into the trees, then once we reached the canopy, using special equipment we had in the van, we were able to move from tree to tree with relative ease. Thus, just where we were in the dark treetops was a mystery to our pursuers.

The mercenaries formed a circle with their backs to one another looking up, then one of them called out, "I see one!" Then he took the first shot at what turned out to be one of a thousand-night shadows. That was his first and last mistake. The Zealot returned fire, and he did not miss. Though the target had on body armor; the Zealot had somehow found a gap in it. From that point it was a fire fight with shots ringing out all over.

We had the advantage, and they knew it, so the seven assailants still standing began to move. But we'd anticipated that they would, so we were prepared for that. Nia sent in her four-legged troops. The local dogs plus two wild coyotes pursued the mercenaries, literally nipping at their heels. Our animal friends pushed the men past Kisha's position, and once they were in front of her, she fired off a series of arrows from her bow, hitting three to four of the men from behind in their legs, beneath their body armor. Kisha called out. "I'm going to ground."

The Heretic replied, "We're right behind you." as he and the Zealot repelled down from their perches.

Since the whirly bird had departed the area, I turned my attention to the next scene we'd staged. But they were nearing the range limit of my thermal imaging device. While it still worked, it allowed me to see both the position of my teammates, in blue (anyone with one of our headsets appeared as blue dots on my screen), and the location of our opponents, in red.

Then seeing what I feared, I called out "Stop! Everybody, stop! They stopped short of the spot." The mercenaries had stopped short of where we needed them to go, for our plan to work. They'd posted up behind several trees, looking to ambush their pursers, Kisha, the Heretic and Zealot.

Then I heard Roughneck's announce on behalf of his team, "Then we'll just go to them."

Sticking my tablet in my backpack, I slung myself down the rope I'd tied to the branch below me so quickly that the rope nearly burned through my gloves. Then after slapping on my infrared enhanced night goggles, I ran towards the commotion, slowing only once I got near. I removed my sidearm and took up a somewhat protected position from which I could see our opponents.

Roughneck, The Russian, Grimes and Nia engaged them from the other side. Having had the element of surprise, however brief it was, allowed Roughneck to sneak up on one of the mercenaries, who literally had his sights trained the other way. If Roughneck gets his hands on you, you're done, as was this black clad fellow was.

Since the men had stopped running, Nia called off her collection of stray canines (for their well-being), and now called on the creatures of the air (owls, hawks and crows) to harass the soldiers, by dive bombing them in the darkness.

We'd had the advantage of surprise and strategy, and had taken out four of them by this point, but that left four bad guys still in play and they were very well dug in. This is when things tend to get hard, and the odds of casualties on our side can become just as high as our opponent.

Then just as I saw another warm body coming across the tree line and obviously headed towards the sounds of gunfire, I heard Voodoo Priestess in my ear, "I'm here. I need for y'all to back." Once we did, the "one who moves without moving" disappeared from sight only reappear in the middle of our remaining opponents. She pulled something pulled something off her waist, and cast it into the air. Then she was gone. Moments later, through my goggles, I saw the mercenaries moving towards one another, as I heard again the sounds of combat, and it was clear that they were attacking one another. In less than five minutes it was over. The men had attacked and killed one another, leaving only one man alive, and he was wounded so severely, that he too was destined for the grave.

By the time I arrived from my position, the air had cleared and Voodoo Priestess was giving the rundown of what had just happened. "So, yeah this stuff basically over stimulates your fear receptors, and it's particularly effective in low light or darkness, when the pattern recognition in our brains see a monster in every shadow and every movement as a threat."

Nia signed to her, asking why it had no effect on her?

Voodoo Priestess answered, "Well, since discovering the plant from which you make this stuff, I've been exclusively using honey from the bees that pollenate it. Thus, by exposing myself to it little by little, I built up an immunity to its effects."

"That technique building resistance was discovered by west Africans and brought America by enslaved peoples." Grimes added.

Voodoo Priestess added, "Indeed. I call this stuff fear dust. Not the most creative name, but it works."

Looking around at the bodies on the ground, Roughneck commented, "Yes, I'd say so."

I stepped over to greet Voodoo Priestess, "Wow!"

She smiled back, "No worries, you know I got you."

"But..." Grimes started, "... they had on bodycams."

I replied, "But it's pitch black in here. We'll have to take one of these with us to check the resolution."

"But for now, we have to assume the worst, so we need to scatter with a quickness. And Blondie, you should already be on a jet out of here." Kisha stated definitively, nodding to The Russian.

The Russian answered, "Understood. I'll reach out when I'm safe."

Grimes, added "I'll go with you."

"No, my love, you know you can't do that. The pair of us traveling together? No, that would make things exponentially more dangerous for us both."

Marketing Girl spoke into our headsets, "I'm on it. Expect confirmation emails to your alias email accounts over the next six hours or so." Marketing Girl knew the protocol of how to sweep our trail. Some of us would be flying charter, some domestic carriers and others would need to bus it out of town to fly out from a regional airport.

Nia touched my shoulder and signed, "What about the bodies?"

The Russian answered, "Their employer will send a crew, probably in the very early morning."

"Oh, really?" Roughneck asked. "I might want to have some fun with them." And actually, he did. In fact, he and a few of his boys were there to "greet" the fake county watershed management duo when they arrived the next morning. He did it just to muck with Entropy and their whole crew. But that's a story for another day.

As we turned and headed towards where Marketing Girl was to pick us up, Voodoo Priestess walked over to The Russian and hugged her tightly. The Russian offered back, "This is what we spoke of that day at the lake, is it not?"

"Yes, I'm afraid so, my dear." they walked towards the van arm in arm. Years later I realized that Voodoo Priestess moved heaven and earth to join us that night, not just me, but also to see The Russian as well. I was swept with the feeling that I'd never see her again, and yet I did.

Grimes, shook his head as he watched The Russian walk away, "That child is delicious, and marvelously so..." That was about as close to expressing love that Grimes could ever possibly be.

Once back at the van, before we all departed, I noticed the glow of Roughneck's old flip phone, as he checked a text. I knew that it was his wife checking in on him, probably having heard about a shootout near the trap house. No, they might not be together, but they were still a pair. Kisha realized this too. And as she stepped to him, chastising him for not using the new encrypted phone we'd long since given him, I knew that what she was really upset about were his ties to his ex.

Perhaps there is no balm for such hard moments, but after giving me a look of exasperation, he spoke to Kisha with pure butter and honey in his voice, "I got this baby, don't you worry 'bout a thing..."

Next: Walking with A Ghost (My Hummingbird – Marketing Girl)

Walking with a Ghost
(Hummingbird)

Dazed and confused on a bed of hot sand, I awoke.
Rolling over, I pushed myself up to a kneeling
position. There I steadied myself before attempting to
come to my feet. In that moment, head lifted, I was struck dumb
by what I saw. As I stood, through waves of black smoke, sandy
grit and a lingering mental haze, I peered up and down the beach
bearing witness to roof tops ablaze in every direction. In the
afternoon sun, an unbearable darkness ruled the sky. It was a
sign, one that, in my blindness, I missed.

As I took breath, the fumes nearly overcame me. What I
smelled was something akin to napalm. Then at last, I began to
remember. I remembered the blast. Something had exploded
very close to me. I had been blown through the door I was
opening from the lobby and onto the boardwalk. In the moment I
reasoned that I'd retained enough sense to head towards the
water. But in truth, I had no recollection of how I'd gotten there.

Gathering myself, I stumbled away from the water and
towards the hell before me. It was off season, and yet I knew that
there had to be others in the building. Dazed as I was, I still
believed that I could be of some help.

But about three steps up the beach I was struck like
lightning from above with the realization that I'd not come to the
beach alone. One of our contractors, Roughneck, had jumped in
the car with me as I departed for the gulf coast. Actually, he
elbowed his way into rolling with me to the beach. He'd never
been to the panhandle of Florida before, so I said sure. But in

truth, I think he wanted to roll with me, because he knew that there was a price on all of our heads, thus he couldn't understand how I could go on vacation by myself? Basically, though he'd never voice it out loud, he was concerned about my well-being. And I was concerned about his wellbeing and that of our whole team. The scene before me, validated our concerns. Through our concern for our community and each other, we'd grown into a family. Thus, my eyes scanned with vigor for him up and down the boardwalk.

Roughneck and I grew up in the same neighborhood and knew the same folks, even though we walked different paths. Growing up, I followed the path demanded of me in my house; college, church and a good job. Roughneck was the local doughboy who rose up through the ranks to run his own crew. But after doing a couple bids, upstate, he left the life, mostly. Regardless, we both had a love for our hood, and found common ground in protecting it. Yes, he was our local hired muscle, but he was more than that. He was truly an equal member in our team.

Stumbling as I reached the stairs, I pulled myself up to the boardwalk running along the rear of the low-rise condo nestled between the multi-million-dollar beach homes. Peering through a smoky corridor, I could see that the local fire crews had arrived and from the parking lot, were pouring water onto the upper floors of the building. I thought to dash through the haze to the apparent safety of the other side, but I was frozen by the thought, "What if Roughneck were somewhere on this side of this blazing hell?" So, I chose to go up and down the boardwalk and pool area just to make sure that Roughneck wasn't lying somewhere, just as I was only minutes before. Pacing back and forth, I thought I saw something in the pool through the haze, so I called out, "Roughneck!"

Then, from behind me, I heard a familiar voice, "Blerd!"

I turned around and saw Roughneck standing there with a huge grin. We both smiled as we greeted one another, happy that we'd both managed to survive the blast. "Where were you dude?" I asked.

"Man, I got knocked into the pool. Thankfully, it was shallow. What about you?"

"I had just got here and was on my way out to the hot tub when the blast hit, so I guess that I got blown over the shrubs and onto the beach." I answered. Shifting, afraid that my lack of certainty regarding what may have actually happened to me might show, I asked, "Hey, looks like Fire and Rescue could use a hand. Do you feel up to it?"

"You already know." the ruffian grinned back. The last time Roughneck served time; he took up the B'hai faith tradition. Lord knows that it was the right path for him. Though, I must say that, even back in the day, he lived by a code. If you weren't in the game, you had nothing to fear from him. Even when he was hustling, he was the kind of brother to step in when he saw something foul going on.

We dashed through one of the smoky corridors to the parking lot beyond. There we saw a single fire truck. It struck me that with blazes up and down the beach, the local fire department was stretched thin. I called out, "Hey chief, could you use a hand?"

The older white-haired man, answered over the noise of the engine and hose, "Yes, I could use some help. Grab that axe down there and check for survivors in each unit, while I try to get this fire under control. We're just not staffed for something like this!" The Fire Chief glanced towards the blazes raging all around us with a heavy sigh.

I took an ax for myself and yelled to Roughneck, "I'll take the units on that side, and you take these!" I rushed to the far stairwell. I figured that since the roof was still very much on fire, that I should start with the units on top floor. So, I ran up to the third floor, and while still panting, I began to sling the ax into the door of the first unit. I only needed to dislodge the lock from the frame enough to gain entrance. Doing so, I then threw my shoulder into the door and it flung open. I rushed in and seeing no one in the living room, I ran to each of the bedrooms, and found them empty as well. But as I returned to the living room on my way out of the unit, I happened to glance out onto the balcony, where I noticed a large odd-looking drone hovering. The next moment, the patio glass door shattered. The drone had fired a shot in my direction. I hit the floor and rolled behind the couch, hoping that if this was simply a remotely controlled drone, and that it wouldn't be able to follow me too far into the interior of the condo without losing connectivity to its pilot. But hearing it buzzing ever closer to my position, I weighed my options. I could make a break for the front door or retreat further into the condo, possibly trapping myself. I opted for the latter, as I knew full well the expected move was for me to bolt for the front door. Seeing the drone's shadow high on the wall in front of me, I knew exactly where it was when I launched myself down the hallway and towards the back bedrooms.

Immediately, I heard the pop, pop of gunfire from the drone's mounted automatic. Thus, though I'd planned to barricade myself in one of the bedrooms, I had no choice but to throw myself into the nearest room, which was the bathroom. I managed to slam the door behind me, and though I knew the drone had no means to turn the doorknob, I locked the door anyway.

Once I heard the craft fire into the door again, I realized a couple of things. I knew then that the drone was AI (Artificial Intelligence) enabled and would attempt to finish out its mission even without its pilot literally calling the shots. Secondly, since I was now bleeding from my arm, I knew that the drone was also capable of thermal imaging, and that its last shot through the door, had grazed my left arm. Putting the pieces together, as I laid there, I also realized that though I had many enemies, only one had the capacity to do something like this. Entropy.

I tumbled over into the bathtub and quickly turned on the shower. Then for extra protection I pulled the shower curtain across the length of the tub. I had no idea how many bullets the craft held, so I couldn't wait it out in that regard. Once the tub was mostly full, I shut off the water for just a moment and laid quiet and still, while I listened. Then I heard it, the whirling of the drone as it hovered just outside of the bathroom door.

The drone then called out in a feminine voice, "Blerd, please come out, we just want to talk. Please open the door." Great, they'd even taught their AI to lie.

Then I looked up again and noticed a small window above the tub. How could I even think that I'd be able to get my broad shoulders through that tiny window? And yet the Universe had left me but one way out, thus it this had to be my path. I turned the shower back on to mask my movements and only then began my ascent. I reached to open the window and as I did a shot rang out. Looking at the hole in the shower curtain, I could see that the drone, sensing a change in the thermal image it perceived due to the window being opened, had fired a shot into and through the window. Naturally, I winced and withdrew my hand from the window, until I understood what had just happened.

After pointing the shower head as high as it would go, I turned back to the small open window. Not being a complete fool, I waved my hand back and forth in front of the window to see if the drone would fire. It did not. Next, I reached up to fully lift the window. Then at last, I stood completely straight up and began to pull myself up. First, I stuck my right arm through the window. Having done that, then came the most challenging part, getting this big old noggin of mine through, while it was still attached to these shoulders of mine. And yet, somehow, I managed. With my head fully through, I looked and listened in the twilight for any sign of the drone. Seeing none, I pulled my torso, hips and legs through the window, while still hanging on to the windowsill. It was a three story drop to sodded soil below. I decided that my best course of action would be to attempt to swing back and forth until I had enough momentum to launch myself back towards the third-floor landing from which I'd entered the unit. If I missed, I'd find out just how soft or not the grass below really was.

I steeled myself and then swung to my right as hard as I could releasing the window sill and grasping for the painted bannister beyond. Of course, gravity was having none of this. As I reached out, my only option was to attempt to grab a hold of one of the vertical wooden beams running from the bannister to the fourth-floor landing. My right hand caught a hold just long enough for my left hand to grab a second beam. As I dangled, struggling to hang on, I heard Roughneck call out, "Blerd!, I got you!" He reached over the bannister and pulled me up and over the beam and onto the landing.

"You heard the shots?" I asked my brother

Roughneck gave me a look which fully, without words, expressed just how stupid a question that was to ask him. Finally, he asked, "So, what's the deal?"

"There's an armed drone inside of that unit, waiting for me to come out of the bathroom. Soon it will realize that I'm not in there, and then come out here looking for me."

"Options?" The bruiser asked.

"Well, I dropped my axe in there, not that bringing a knife, no matter how large, to a gun fight would have been a good idea. We could run, but bursting out into the open could play right into its hands."

"And running only delays things anyway. Do you know who did this? Knowing your opponent is a basic tenant of warfare. Who would want us dead this bad, bad enough to do this?" Roughneck waved his arms cautiously towards all of the collateral damage.

"I think Entropy did this. Best guess is that a larger drone dropped an ordinance on this building targeting us. The second drone was to verify the kill and take action if need be. Torching the other places along the beach was merely a cover."

"So, you think they did all of this, just to get us? That's not their style. They survive by staying in the shadows."

"True that. But it is like Entropy to influence people and events. I could see them influencing some poor sap looking to make a statement, to pick this location, on this day. But if I had to guess, the smaller drone is the only direct connection to Entropy."

"Really? And, they just knew that we'd be here this weekend? Nah. You're twisting over backwards for that one. The truth, when you find out the real deal, will be something right in your face. It will be simple and plain."

Clearly, I was missing something.

"No, you're right. But it's got to be something."

Roughneck, repeating a refrain, he'd often said to me, "And what good would knowing that something do you right now?" My dear brother's unspoken mantra was to live in the moment, and as a product of the streets where death was always just a breath away, there was no other path. "I know you're worried about the others and what does this all means? And if we are compromised, by how much? But understand this first and foremost, if you don't survive this moment, you'll be of no help to them. So, what do we need to do now to see another day?"

"Take out that drone."

"And how do we do that?"

I thought for a moment, before taking note that the middle units had ceiling to floor windows along the back walkway, instead of the private balconies that the outside units had. But more importantly, the lighting was such that my reflection could be seen in the glass pane, as I hid behind one of the outside structural beams. I pointed towards the glass, and then over my shoulder past the balcony, gesturing in a way to convey to Roughneck, what I was doing.

If the drone were to pass through the line of sight in which I saw the mirage of a beach, that drone instead would see an image of me. I stood there in stillness, for what seemed an eternity, and yet my heart quickened, when at last I heard the buzzing of the killer drone as it departed from the unit I'd escaped. It had flown out of the same glass balcony door it had shattered and was now floating towards my position scanning the walkway. As it buzzed along, behind my position, I held my breath. Then at last it reached the point where my reflection was surely cast. It pulled in for a better shot as I'd hoped. Then as my flying would-be assassin passed over the railing, I lunged grabbing a hold of the drone from behind with both hands. I slung it as forcibly as I could into the concrete walkway with bad intent, repeatedly.

"That's spirit, brother!" Roughneck shouted.

Because of the adrenalin coursing through my veins, it took a minute for me to comprehend that I'd eliminated the threat. Still breathing heavily, I mustered up a "Yeah..."

After I gathered myself, we proceeded back down to where we'd come, checking each unit for survivors, breaking the occasional window and door to be sure. Between the moments, as we descended, Roughneck spoke to me. "Brother, I've found in life, that the truth of things is always right in front of us, if we only have eyes to see it." As we turned the corner and descended the last set of steps, he continued. "But until we are willing to accept a truth, we will always be blind to it. Sure, you guys all got new identities, packed up and moved away, after

Money was murdered, but are you really any safer? Retreat is tactic, not a strategy."

Reaching the ground level, we stood in front of the pool once more. "I know. I just didn't want lose anyone else. But I realize now that this is not sustainable."

"Yes. Play it this way and all you'll do is delay the inevitable. In the meantime, Entropy will get each of us one by one. And until then, all of us will live each day in fear, waiting to die. What kind of life is that? Or instead, you can face these cats head on! Yeah, it's very likely that may cost you lives too, maybe all your lives. But if any of you survives long enough to live a single day without fear, those will be priceless days."

"Damn. You're right, I've been trying to deal with E on my own, while everyone else remains in the shadows."

"Trust your team. That doesn't mean ignoring their faults." As Roughneck said these words, I noticed a partially burnt flip phone lying on the pool deck. In an instant I realized that it was Roughneck's old phone. Not the new phone I'd bought him with tech to make it untraceable. He paused for a moment, giving me a sorry bro look. Entropy had tracked us via Roughneck's old phone. In that moment the scales fell from my eyes, and I noticed a body floating face down in the pool. At last, I knew exactly who it was. Then Roughneck's smiled at me. "Brother Blerd, if you remember nothing else, remember what you once said to me, you don't defeat the darkness, by hiding your light, but rather by being the light that banishes it. As I tilted my head looking at him, I saw him become translucent. Then as he started to ascend from me, he began to shimmer in hues of yellow, green and blue and he smiled even more broadly as he transformed, until he was, at last, a hummingbird. For a long moment, he hovered looking back at me. Then in a single move, he turned and flew towards the western sun as I lost him in the light and found my own path.

Epilogue: I uploaded the A.I. I'd been working on for so long into the cloud the following day. Game on.

The Girl Part Two

Okay, so I'm happy to report that things are looking up. I hadn't been punched, shoved or spat on in nearly 72 hours (It was almost as if the universe had declared some sort of three-day holiday truce). Of course, I'd been called a few things, many of which I didn't understand (language and phrasing are evolving so fast these days that I can't keep up), but always understood, if only by their tone, the intent of their words. But despite my low standing within the social hierarchy, amazingly I'm driving my girlfriend, yes, my *girlfriend*, to take her state of Georgia driving test (it's a true miracle that such a word as "girlfriend" could ever occupy a space within my consciousness, and much less my spoken vocabulary). Although my friend Itchy, questioned the whole "friend" aspect of that term; given that she offered me up to her former coven as a human sacrifice. So, I can see why he might feel that way. He said, "Scratchy, dude don't you realize that homicidal partners can be, shall we say, *problematic*...?" True, but can there truly be love without pain? Besides the seemingly random oozing on my cheek (one of those witches bit me so hard, that she put a hole in my cheek, and it got infected, and I can't afford to get it looked at), life is pretty good.

So, as we approached the DMV, I saw my girl pull out a pair of glasses from her purse, and slap them on her face. "What are those?" I asked.

"Oh, I don't need 'em. I only wear them when I'm taking a driving test."

And like the fool I am, I didn't have sense enough, not to inquire further (willful ignorance is highly underrated, in fact, it's quickly becoming my drug of choice). "Huh, what do you mean? Like you see okay, but you wear them for the test, just to be sure?"

"Well, see the thing is, I'm pretty much legally blind, according to the bureaucrats. But what do they know? A little bit of schooling don't make you smart, life does. And I've lived a lot of it in my few short years."

And damnit, once again, I didn't have the discipline to keep my mouth shut (must be some undiagnosed form of turrets). "But you do have a license, I've seen it."

"Of course, I do. In fact, I have a lot of them, but they're all suspended. So, I need a new one. That's part of the reason I moved to Georgia, because I haven't had one here before. All I need to do is to spell my name a little differently, put on these glasses and I'm good for the test. No Problem." The irony here being that I know how to drive, but have no license, while the Girl who doesn't know how to drive, has a purse full of them.

At last I realized why this beautiful girl was with me, beyond my doing whatever she asked. She was legally blind. And truth be told, I was cool with it. I'd been in a couple of car accidents with her by this point, not counting the times that she ran into inanimate objects (stop signs, fire hydrants, and two mimes). And sure, there were other clues, but I just assumed that she was poorly coordinated. I mean, we don't all dance, and we don't all sing, so it stands to reason that some of us can't drive or recognize stop signs when we blow by them. But it never occurred to me that she couldn't see. But I realized quickly that it was best not to tell anyone this fact, lest my position as number one lacky to the blind queen be usurped.

After dropping the girl off at the DMV entrance, I parked the car in the staging area for her. The front of the building was all glass, so I had a front row seat to all the happenings. The first person she encountered, when her number was called was a woman. The Girl presented her documentation, despite how little it was, to the woman. But I could clearly see that she wasn't buying it. Then it was apparent to me, that the Girl asked for a manager. So, I saw the older woman manager join the two of them. The Girl glanced out through the glass in my direction making a sad face. The three of them conversed some, before the director of that location was called over. He happened to be a middle-aged black man, with a little bit of a gut. I don't know if the Catholic Church would agree with me, but I witnessed a modern-day miracle that day. The director guffawed and carried on so, that I was embarrassed for my entire gender. Side note: I noticed that the entire indoor office staff was female, except for the director (and I'd be willing to bet that at least one or two of those women were better educated than the director) and the brother working outside maintenance. But the state assigned troopers to perform the actual driving tests that day, were no more diverse; three older white guys and an older white woman. The DMV in any state, will tell you all you need to know about that state. So, if you're thinking about relocating, visit the DMV first. That is what you're in for. I'm just saying...

From the bench upon which I sat during her test, I could see clearly that she drove over several cones, ran at least one stop sign (even with her glasses on), and was very crooked at the end of her parallel parking attempt. Once they pulled back up to the starting line, she and the officer sat in the car several long minutes. When they exited, the Girl walked towards me with an all so subtle look of victory on her face that she tried to suppress, as the officer returned to his post. The Girl, before reentering the main building, paused as she opened the door, giving me a "wow" look with her mouth hanging wide open. She'd "passed" her driving test. Like me, these poor souls at the DMV never had a chance. But I knew the odds where in her favor, when I saw that three of the four examiners were men, and given the Girl's skills, many a woman too would have bent to her will. The lone woman examiner walked slowly by me with a look of disgust on her face, but still she didn't cross that thin blue line.

So, the Girl sashayed out of the building as I walked over to meet her at the car. I casually offered to drive (I'm a fool, but not a complete one), and she consented. After screaming in joy as we pulled away from the facility, she announced, "Hey, I need to make a stop."

"Sure, where at?"

"It's around Greenbriar." Going totally analog, she hands me a piece of paper with an address hand written on it.

"Okay…" I knew the street, so I hopped onto the expressway, and proceeded to southwest Atlanta. But as we pulled up to the spot, I could see clearly that it was a trap house, with a couple of dough boys posted up on the front porch. The word, "Really?" convulsed through my lips, without my conscious approval.

"What?" She asked, genuinely confused.

I threw both of my arms forwards with my palms up in exasperation, while I looked back and forth between her and the dope house, knowing that neither one of us was about *this* life. Hell, I get nervous just playing trap music with the windows down.

"What?" she asked again, in what appeared to be genuine confusion. Bless her beautifully ignorant heart.

A moment later, the front door burst open and a big burley brother strode out with his arms spread wide and darn near shouting, "My girl!"

"Hi Dilton!"

I leaned in towards the Girl as the big man approached, "So, what kind of name is Dilton?"

"His name is Dilton, Dilton Mavis. I think he's from West India."

She meant the West Indies, but I didn't bother to correct her. So, dude asks right off, "Who is this Nigga?" Immediately, from the way he said it, I knew that Dilton was really from Decatur.

"Oh, he's my mentee."

For half a second, I glance at her, but quickly realized that it might be in my best interest to just play along.

"Did you tell him about the job?"

"Of course, not."

Then Dilton gave me a second look as he rubbed the fuzz on his chin, "But maybe he can be a lookout, you feel me?"

"Lookout???" I thought to myself, as I maintained my silence and my gaze towards the ground directly in front of me.

Then he decided, "Throw him in the back seat and let's roll!" As Dilton started the car he looked over to the Girl, and announced to the universe, "Look at her… Nobody is gonna be checking for her. She's perfect!"

So, as we rolled out, Dilton is driving, the Girl is in the front passenger seat, and I'm sitting in the rear middle seat, between two armed bangers. I know that I should have been in fear for my life, but since I'd pretty much given up on a happy ending for myself years ago, I knew that things would end badly for me, only the details remained to be experienced. Yeah, I pretty much figured I'd punchout of this life during some such bullshit. Hash tag, *hood-life*.

Just as we were about to turn the last corner towards our destination, Dilton brought the car to a full stop. But even from there, I knew our target. They'd said it was one of those payday loan stores, you find all over the hood, but we were in Midtown? "Okay, little man, this is where you hop out. Take this with you. Just press the button on the side to talk. If you see the po-po, just press the button and say nine, one, one. You don't need to say anything else. Got it?"

"Yes, sir."

"Sir..?" Dilton laughed, as did his cohorts in the backseat. Then still laughing, he added, "Git your ass out of this car!"

So, there I stood, as they pulled away with the Girl. The car pulled slowly down the street, and into a parking spot (Dilton was actually a very good parallel parker; he got it on one try) right in front of the small financial institution.

Okay, full disclosure, if you live in the "A" this is like remedial, but as we rode out, I had just assumed we'd be going to Candler Road, Old National Highway, or one of many avenues of commerce in black Atlanta (all the places that charge an APR of 100% plus, are located in the hood). So, I was shocked to see that we were in the all so affluent Midtown. That being the case, I knew for sure, that this endeavor was not going to go well. But like my life, just how badly things would turn out was the only real question. I was simply curious about just how mucked up I'd be when all of this ended? If you're a betting man, always take the over when it comes to the amount of calamity in my life.

Anyway, the crew got out, while the Girl slid over to the driver's seat. Actually, that was the one thing they got right, no one would try a woman that beautiful. She looked like she belonged, she had the gear, the look, all that. She'd dressed that morning for conquest, and in that regard, she was winning.

Although I was down the street from the bank, I was able to follow the happenings over the two-way. So, as I'm listening in, I hear the following.

"Sir, we're an online bank. We don't carry any cash here."

"What? That doesn't make any sense. How can you be a bank, and not have any money?"

"Well, we do have money technically, we just don't have any cash."

I heard one of the doughboys chime in, "Dilton, all I hear is double talk from this fool. I say we waste his ass, and see if that loosens up any lips!"

Then I heard a woman's voice. "Sir, I'm customer service, perhaps I can assist you better."

"That's more like it." Dilton replied in relief.

Then the woman spoke again, "Though, as the sign says, we have no cash at this branch, that doesn't mean that you can't get paid."

Dilton nodded, "Keep talking..."

"I'd be happy to transfer funds to your account from my own personal account. Do you happen to know your bank account number, or do you have personal check on you? I can get the number from that."

Frustrated, Dilton replied, "Who in the hell memorizes their bank account numbers? And no, I don't have any checks on me." Then I heard Dilton ask, "Do either of you?" which I assumed was directed towards his boys. I heard soft no's come back across the airwaves.

Then the woman spoke again. "That's okay, that's okay..." she tried to reassure Dilton and his crew. "Do you have Cash App or Paypal" By the absence of sound coming back, I imagined the three would be bank robbers staring at one another.

At last Dilton broke the silence, "No, we don't."

"I take it you don't have an account with any of the major crypto currencies?" she asked.

"What? Krypto? Ain't that Superman's dog or something?"

Then, and I have to hand it to Ms. Customer Service lady, she came up with a very clever solution while the rest of the staff was apparently crapping their pants.

"Let's do this then. Let's open up an account for you using your social, and I'll personally transfer a couple of grand into it, to get you started."

Then one of the banker bros spoke up, "Awesome idea Aisha. You do that and I'll add to it, and I'm sure that the others will too." I heard a chorus of two or three other voices agreeing to the plan."

I could hear Dilton and crew adding different versions of "That's alright."

One of the doughboys added, laughing, "And I thought for sure that I was going to have to pop a cap in somebody's ass up in here."

But of course, it couldn't be that easy. Over the two way, I heard, "Who are they?"

"Who are who, sir?" I heard this Aisha reply back.

"Those folks at the door with their cell phones out?"

"Oh, those are our customers. I guess they're trying to figure out what's going on. I mean, y'all did lock the door, but left the *Open* sign up."

One of the dough boys called out, "Dilton, these fools out here filming us!"

"Ah, hell no!" the wannabe gangster said aloud.

Then as I'm hearing thugs one and two getting amped up, I heard Aisha say, "Sir, please sit back down, we're almost done." There was a pause, then I heard her say, "...and no matter how this goes, don't you want to at least get paid?"

"Damn girl, you the kind of woman a nig…, a man needs in his life."

So, it was at that same moment, that I saw a police car pull up with two cops jumping out, and a third officer running down the street towards the bank. Then I shouted frantically, "The police, the police, nine, one, one…!!!" I heard some commotion then saw the glass front door shatter and the hotheaded dough boy run out shooting indiscriminately. He ran to the getaway car and pulled quickly on the door handle twice as he screamed for the Girl to unlock the door, but instead, she peeled away from the curb nearly taking the young man with her. After regaining his balance, the gunman ran off with one of the officers in hot pursuit.

As for the Girl, she executed a U-turn, well actually it was more like a W-turn, since she did hit a light pole and a car parked on the other side of the street. Then either by chance or intent, I saw her screaming down the road towards me. I assumed that she was coming to pick me up. But as she approached, instead of pulling up along the curb, she headed right towards me. Her car jumped the curb and nailed me before I had a chance to jump out of the way. I flew back and into a restaurant dumpster. That green monster had zero give.

Oblivious to my pain, all she said, over and over again, was "Let's go…!"

Although, I knew that I had several broken bones (what was straight, was now bent), I dragged myself to the rear driver's side door, and began to pull myself in. But before I could complete the task, the Girl threw the car into reverse, with my legs not yet in the vehicle. I screamed in pain. Then she stopped to put the car into drive, as she did, I made one final pull to secure my place. The door slammed shut as she hit the accelerator.

"I think I need to go to the emergency room!" I cried.

"What? We need to need to get gone, like lost, real quick. You can see the doctor tomorrow! Right now, we need to get off these busy streets. Here, you drive!"

At that announcement, she pulled the car over and dragged me from the backseat and into the driver's seat. Though my left leg was clearly broken, my right leg was still functioning. But bending my left leg enough to fit into the driver's seat was an excruciating pain even for someone like me with a very high pain tolerance. But somehow, I managed to get us onto the expressway.

The Girl commanded, "Take me to my house, then you can Uber home.

So, as we're driving, she whipped out her cell phone to take a selfie, and she did it in such a way as to include me in the shot. Then she dictated the caption into her phone, "Me and my getaway driver leaving the scene! Hashtag, blood and guts everywhere!"

Then it struck me, this whole day, getting her license, agreeing to drive for Dilton, her even stopping to pick me up as she ran from the scene, was all about her social media following. She'd done it all for the Gram. Damn. Just damn. But sadder still, in spite of who I knew her to be, never once did it occur to me to run like hell. Well, in my condition I couldn't run much of anywhere. However, in hindsight, I guess even hobbling into the nearest abyss, would have been far safer than riding shotgun with this Girl.

Hammer of the Odds

At first thought, you'd think that the odds of actually tracking a pack of flying monkeys would be slim to none. But in truth, it's really not that difficult. It's kind of like tracking down a politician; just follow the shit. The fact that their poop was bright green with purple specks, was very helpful. No, the issue was the terrain. Since the day I awoke in this strange land, I knew that the Cartel maintained a campus up in the hills, and I knew right away, that if I wanted to live a long life here, I'd best keep my ass downtown in the lowlands. I can't say that I'm the brightest guy, but I do have some sense. Well, at least I did.

As I ascended into the hills, railroad hammer in tow, I had to cross streams, climb nearly shear rocks and fight my way through mile after mile of tangled vines. I did this, all the while trying to be unseen, as much as any large black man with a huge hammer strapped to his back could be.

Eventually, I got close enough to take in the Cartel's compound. I saw four or five buildings and a front gate. On the gate was the number "13", which was their official name, though the locals simply referred to them as "The Cartel". Still, as I often did when I saw their legal name, I wondered, "The thirteenth what? And what happened to the other twelve? I mean it does seem to beg the question, right?"

These bastards had kidnapped my girl Carla, to settle a debt against her uncle Chuck. He was the kind of lightweight would-be tough guy who believed himself to be some kind criminal mastermind. But when you're dealing with real criminals, you can't start drinking your own Kool-Aid. My daddy used to tell me, "Son, don't out kick your coverage. So, don't start feeling yourself, thinking you're gonna outsmart the room. That ain't your gift, son. It's better if you just assume that you don't know shit." But waist deep Kool-Aid drinking Chuck owed everybody, and had multiple parties wanting him dead. My bringing him the head of the City Mole, was supposed to be his big come up. In addition, the Collectors, who are these ghostly invisible vigilantes who gather up folks with soiled karma, had him on their "to do list". However, he figured that if he could appease the rulers of the City by killing the "mole" who held their secrets, not only would the powers that be, pay him a nice reward (which he'd used to pay off the Cartel), they'd also decree that the Collectors should leave him be. That would allow him time and coin enough to arrange safe passage into the Lush (word on the street was that the Collectors could not venture into the Lush). But see, old boy Chuck had out kicked his coverage and then some. He thought himself a player, when really, he was just another scrub.

The Collectors had him hemmed him up in his office just as I arrived to collect my pay for killing the mole. The bracelet I'd found in the sewers allowed me to see these "ghosts" even though they should have been invisible to me. The whole scene was surreal. But I played it cool, pretending that I only saw Chuck, and without a word I grabbed the envelope with my 5000 credits and backed out. But just as I escaped Chuck's trailer with my fee and my life, I saw a pack of winged monkeys from the Cartel flying off with Carla. The bastard had offered his niece as collateral for the loan they'd made him. In truth, they'd hoped that Chuck would default, given Carla's psychic gifts. The Cartel, was more than willing to have the talented Carla instead.

Lying there in the overgrowth outside of the Cartel compound, I realized that I had two problems. First, I had no clue as to where they might be holding Carla. Secondly, I was only armed with a hammer. A rather large hammer, used to lay rail (which is what I do), but still at the end of the day, it was still just a hammer.

But then I remembered the bracelet I wore. In the sewer and back in Chuck's office, it allowed me to see whatever it was that I needed to see at the time. Thus, as I looked back and forth across the campus, I saw an image through one of the outer walls, of someone bound to a chair. I knew that this was my Carla. So, all I had to do then, was to get past their security undetected, then somehow break into the building in which she was being held, and get her to safety, going up against a militia armed with future tech weapons that could literally vaporize me. As you can see, I'd not really thought this through. Which is par for the course with me (sleeping with my landlady, taking a gig to bag a giant mole-woman roaming the sewers and risking my life to rescue some skirt I'd just met). I'm not known for planning things out. But as my daddy used to say, "Just because you're not smart, doesn't mean that you have to be stupid." Rescuing a woman, I'd just met certainly wasn't a smart thing to do, yet a vague rescue plan entered my head. Which basically meant that, once again, I hadn't thought it all the way through.

Being of man of action, I wasn't the kind of man to hesitate once I had my mind made up. So, after I buried away my hard-earned reward money beneath the kudzu, I exited from overgrowth and stepped onto the road leading up to the campus.

I walked up to the front gate with both hands held high. I called out to the two guards standing there, "Hey, I'm John."

One of the guards replied, "John?"

"John H."

"John H, what?"

"Just John H."

"Okay, bruh. What you want?"

"Y'all know that junkyard guy named Chuck?"

The two guards looked at one another, and snickered just a bit. "Yeah…" they both said.

The first one then offered, "I just heard that the Collectors got him."

The other one laughed and added, "Yeah, poor Chuck."

"Well, he owed me money, 'cause I killed that mole which supposedly didn't exists, but really did. Chuck hired me to kill it, I did, so he owes me a payday for doing it, a big one."

"Who didn't he owe? A lot of folks are going to be fighting over the scraps in his yard. But what does that have to do with us?"

"Well, one of the workers down there told me that y'all collected on his debt. I figured that I ought to get a cut of that."

One of the men answered, "Really???"

The other man laughed "So, you want us to cut off one of her fingers and give it to you?"

"No, but I feel like I ought to get something, from somebody."

"One of the men pointed his gun at me, "So, you bringing that foolishness to the one three?" Until that moment I had not considered that there might be some sort of implied hyphen or comma between those digits, pasted all over town. Dude added, "Get the hell on away from here with that bullshit!"

Then the other man, pressing the nozzle of his partner's gun down, laughed and said softly, "I think the boss might get a good laugh out of this fool."

So, after taking away my hammer (I must really, really love this woman to give up my hammer; but I'd never felt a connection like this before), they led me away into the complex. Soon enough, they'd pointed, poked and pushed me along to the same building where I knew they were holding Carla, as I'd hoped they might.

They tied me to a chair, and called the boss man. As he entered the room, one of the guards offered, "Jaheim, this is the dude."

Laughing Jaheim asked, "So, let me get this straight, you want me to pay you, because old Chuck, old grimy Chuck got collected before you got paid?"

I tilted my head, "Well, yeah..."

All three of the men burst out laughing gut busting laughs, with one of them actually rolling on the floor.

Jaheim who was laughing so hard, that he found it hard to formulate words, "So, hold up, you came up here, to the Cartel, asking us to pay you, what Chuck owed you?"

"Well, I wasn't thinking that you'd pay all of it, but I thought y'all could pay a brother something. Enough for me not to get put out my place at least?" That last part was true, in that I'd signed up for this City Mole snipe hunt to avoid being put out. "You know, like maybe 10,000 credits…" I may not be smart, but on the chance that they did pay me, I thought I'd double the price.

Jaheim, pointed at me, laughing, "You know that you fucked up coming up here asking us some bullshit like this, right? The only thing we're thinking about is whether we should whack you here or somewhere else?"

Then, as I replied to Jaheim, I met his eyes, "But, as the one who found the mole and as the one who found her lair and knows where it is, might not the City leaders be interested in speaking to me, before you or anyone whacks me?"

The real reason that there was a bounty on the head of the mole, was that she, the product of genetic experimentation, by a previous generation of City scientists, had been breaking into the homes and vaults of the living and long since dead City elders over the years, collecting their secrets.

I could see in Jaheim's eyes, that at last he realized, that I might have value.

Jaheim engaged his phone to call Chuck's junkyard. At last, getting someone on the line whom he knew would keep his mouth shut, Jaheim asked for a description of the "hero" who'd gone into the sewer and killed the eight-foot tall mole. "Yeah, that's right a big goofy looking Mofo." After disconnecting the call, he turned to me. "Congratulations, the streets know who you are. But I don't know if that changes your situation."

I nodded, "Yeah, but what do you lose by checking up the food chain first?"

Not saying a word, but obviously conceding the point, Jaheim motioned towards his boys, and they all left the room to presumably make some calls. Given that the bracelet allowed me to see through walls, not only did I see my captors discussing things with some unknown third party, I could also see that Carla was being held in the room next to mine.

Now, I told y'all before, like my daddy, I'm a railroad man. But Pops was also a locksmith, which he took up when he got too old to swing the hammer. He told me one day, "Boy, I see your future already, and it's cursed 'cause you were born with that hustling spirit in ya. So, let me teach you something that I know you'll actually use... but don't tell your mama." (Daddy also told me not to tell mama that he was delivering mail to Ms. Jasmine, when I saw him coming out of her house on my way to school one morning, but that's a story for another day). Turns out he was right. So, given the kind of predicaments that always seem to find me, I keep a pin pushed carefully into the back of my leather belt. Thus, though my cuffs were locked behind my back in the high back chair, in less than a minute, I'd managed to pull the long pin from its hiding place. Then, in a moment which would have brought a tear to daddy's eyes, I picked the lock on my handcuffs in seconds.

I wanted to just bolt into the hallway, dash into Carla's room, snatch her up and make a run for it. But then I took a hard look at the window in my room, and remembered that people don't tend to lock upstairs windows. Standing, I quietly grabbed my hammer and strapped it to my back as I moved to the window. It was indeed unlocked, so, I climbed through it.

Standing on the windowsill, while stretching my left foot towards Carla's window, I prayed that no one on the ground would happen to look my way in the fading twilight. Somehow, I managed to pull myself over to Carla's window. I tapped on her window to get her attention. She returned my forced smile, with a look of horror. I replied back with a thumbs up, although a thumbs up in the City, suggested that the recipient of said gesture, stick it up their bum. The fact was that while they spoke English, Chinese and Swahili in the City, it seemed like everything else was completely different from the world I left. Well, almost everything. Seeing Carla and her fine self, reminded me of one thing that will never change.

Once in her room, I moved quickly to free Carla from her cuffs. She stood to hug me and the moment her skin touched mine, I felt that connection, I'd felt only with her, as she spoke directly into my mind without having to say a word. In a fraction of a second, without words, I learned that the Cartel's plan for Carla was to have her be a greeter at some posh bar, where wealthy men go to stare at beautiful women, imagining what they'd never actually do. But with little more than a touch, Carla could snatch their banking passwords from the recesses of their minds (very rich men don't write their most valuable password down).

As she pulled back, still holding my hands, I heard her asking what my plan was to get us to safety? Instantly, she realized that I had no plan. But I don't think she needed to be a mind reader to have known that, it was likely written all over my face. Then we both looked at the window. Walking over to it, I commented softly, "We're only on the second floor. I think we can do this. I'll go first, then I'll help you get down."

So, I climbed out the window and quickly realized, that by this being a commercial building, the first-floor ceiling was going to be twelve or so feet high. Grabbing a hold of the window sill, I dangled for a moment then let go. I landed on my feet and rolled just a bit, bruising my butt in the process. Then it was Carla's turn. She was clearly afraid to let go. So, I'm motioning more and more frantically, for her to just let go, and I'd catch her. Then at last she let go. Okay, let me stop here to explain that I heard a noise behind me just as she was letting go of the ledge, so I turned my head just for a fraction of a second. Anyway, she hit the hard ground with a thud, and worse yet, cried out "Ow...!!!"

I ducked down behind the bushes, grabbing a hold of Carla and covering her mouth to muffle her cries, as her unblinking eyes gave me a what-the-hell stare. I tried to see if any of the guards or random thugs heard anything. I could see them looking around trying figure out where that "strange noise" came from.

Since my skin was touching hers, Carla was able to project her thoughts into me. "You can remove your hand from my mouth now." As she held my hand, I felt her searching my mind. I felt her saying back to me, "So, you still have no plan?"

I stared blankly at her, which is fairly typical of me. I couldn't help but think, "Was I suppose to be coming up with a plan??? I'm a man of..."

"Yes, I can see that you're a man of action. But planning..., not so much, hmm?" A moment passed and I felt us agreeing that whatever we did, should done after dark.

So, we huddled there for twenty minutes or so, waiting for night to take firm hold. Suddenly I felt her pull her hand away from mine, and audibly say, "What! You're thinking about that now?"

I shrugged, as she retook my hand. In quick succession she realized that her breathing, her sweat, and even her gazing at me in disbelief, made me, you know… Well, if you're a dude, you know what I mean. And yet, despite it all, that moment still wouldn't crack my top ten of most embarrassing moments. Hey, it was sleeping with my landlady, my *married* landlady, that led to all of this in the first place (she the one with a husband, but clowning me for being unfaithful… well that, and I'm behind the rent). Bad Choices might as well be my middle name.

Carla regained her poise long enough to take ahold of my hand so that she could quietly share her plan with me. When they brought her in and tied her to the chair, I'd freed her from, she was in contact with her captors long enough to learn their shipping schedule. From the basement of this very building they'd load up drivers with that crap they sell on the streets. Carla was thinking that we could stow away on one of those trucks before it pulled out, if we could sneak into the basement overnight.

"But how do we get into the basement?" I wondered.

Carla replied, "Well, I'd planned to use the stairs, before you had me jump out the window. But look, you see these grates lining the bottom of this wall? They're ventilation for the basement."

"…and too small for either of us to fit though."

"No doubt," She replied, "but if you and your handy hammer can somehow dislodge one of the cinderblocks beside or above the vent, we could." Then somehow, she saw an image in my mind of me swinging my hammer into the block. "No! You'll have to do this quietly, once everyone has turned in for the night. I'll look out for the patrols, while you dig into the cement."

Seemed like a reasonable plan. Yeah, but for that very reason things didn't go as planned. First off two of the flying monkeys posted up next to the bushes in which Carla and I were hiding. One of them broke out a couple of cigarettes, and lighted one for each of them. So, that was a thing.

We laid there for some time, all the while I had the nearly irresistible urge to ask them, since when do monkey's, flying ones in fact, smoke? And not that I would have been able to understand their answer, but given that we only get so many turns around this yellow star (well, if we were still on Earth), some questions simply have to be asked of the Universe, even if the answer is darkness and silence. As my daddy told me, sometimes it the questioning which opens doors, not the answers. I never really understood what he meant until that moment. Things tend to get really clear when your life is on the line. And course, smoking and drinking like they were, one of them had to drop a duce to funk up the place.

Anyway, using the pick side of my hammer, I'd dug through most of the cement molding along the top of the cinder block I'd chosen, when I heard a voice from the other side. Not like from the dead or anything, but from some dude down below in the basement, "What the hell???"

Without hesitation in one fluid motion, I rose to my feet, extracted my hammer and swung it into the cinderblock with all my might. The block flew from its location and into our unseen opponent down below. I could see that Carla was astonished, frustrated and panicked all within the same breath. I shrugged my shoulders, "It's what I do. I hammer things."

Knowing that we'd likely gained unwanted attention, we had to accelerate our timeline. We scurried through the newly opened hole. I went first, and then lowered Carla down into my arms. This was their garage, and it was full of cars and trucks ready to make the rounds at first light, or what passes for morning in The City. Carla said tersely, "Follow me…"

She ran to a desk on the other side of the room and opened the cabinet. She grabbed one of the keys hanging there. She pushed a button, and announced, "That one."

I got behind the wheel, while Carla jumped into the passenger seat. I started the vehicle and slammed the peddle to the floor. We crashed through the garage door nearly running over two guards, as we made a beeline for the same checkpoint gate through which I'd entered this compound. As we rolled down the driveway Carla pulled out one of those new-fangled guns they use in this place and began firing at the guard post. Those guards scattered like roaches when the lights come on. "Damn, girl! You're a real one, huh?"

"You had doubts?" For me monogamy had always sounded too much like monotony. But this woman had me rethinking my position.

As we headed down the road, I have to admit for half a second, I thought about circling back to retrieve the reward money I'd buried in the mountain's overgrowth. But there was zero chance that anyone would discover where I buried it.

"So, where we going?" I asked.

"Away from here, but you're driving, you tell me."

"Well, we just shot up the place, so we'll need to disappear for a minute."

"True. But I've heard tale of this place they call the Lush, where you're out of the reach of anyone or anything from the City."

"Cool. So, you know how to get to this place?"

"Yes, I've known for some time where it's supposed to be. But it seems that today is the day I'll find out if the stories are true."

As I drove, between giving directions, Carla shared secretes about the City that she's learned over the years. "Yeah, so basically, we're floating on a planetoid in space around a star. But what I don't know is the biggest question of all. Did we come here of our own free will, or were we, and are we, simply interned here as a part of some sort of punishment? Did we leave or were we cast out?"

Even my simple mind understood the distinction she was making and its importance. "Yes, sometimes *why* does matter. In this case, it would literally make all the difference in the world."

"Look at you, John; waxing deep and all."

I smiled. We drove through the night and most of the next day. But just an hour or so, before darkness fell, we reached our destination. We knew because, we saw fruit trees everywhere growing wild. As we left the road and drove through the bush, we saw streams, flowers and a canopy so lush, that we understood in full why this place was called *the Lush*.

I was going to stop so that we could exit the truck and just take in what we were seeing, but Carla said, "No, keep going. There should be something else up here that I think you'll want to see."

We drove on for another twenty minutes until at last we reached a clearing. Carla said to me, "Look down there…"

From the lengthen shadows, I took in a sight, I'd not seen in this world. Below us was beach. A beach with white sand, like they have along the Florida panhandle back on the world of my birth. We got out of the truck and trekked down the hillside and onto the beach. We stood in amazement for a few moments before we both plopped down into the sand in awe of the setting binary stars. Carla looked at me, and I knew, I just did. I reached out to pull her near. We kissed. Making love to her was truly unlike making love to anyone else, given that it was making love with no filter. Meaning, that I could tell instantly, what she was truly feeling and likewise she could sense without doubt what was pleasing to me. I knew right then that I never wanted to be apart from this woman ever again.

As the stars at last hit the horizon, Carla sprung to her feet, and darted out into the water, while I sat there laughing. Reaching the water, she called to me, "Come on, before it gets too dark!"

She'd gone out a ways, deep enough to tread water. I'd not been swimming since I woke up in The City, but I wasn't gonna let her play me for no punk. So, I took off my shoes and stood up.

I still remember when it happened. I was smiling as I sauntered towards the waves, when I saw something moving through the water towards Carla. I called out "Carla!!!" But in an instant, she was swallowed up by a real-life Leviathan which breached the water's surface before diving back into the oblivion from which it arose. I yelled, "No...!!!" Then looking up to the heavens, I cried out, "This is some bullshit!"

It was only then that I realized why no one had ever come back from the Lush. Yes, it is beyond the reach of the City, but there are creatures here who have a taste for human flesh. And this one had just taken the one perfect thing I'd found, in my entire life. But since my life meant nothing without her, I grabbed my hammer and dashed into the water. I'd either find her, or die trying...

Behind Brown Eyes

Behind brown eyes, I see.

Stolen identities, broken promises, revisionist history.

No amount of assimilation, acquiescence or achievement can remove this stain.

No raging words, wars or worlds can assuage this pain.

Damned before birth into this mortal world.

Damned since birth to bear the sins of this mortal world.

An empire built upon the backs of our ancestors.

An empire collapsing upon the heads of our children.

The never-ending debt of brown skin.

The eternal blank check strung around our black necks.

Why do the assailed pay the bill?

Why do the beneficiaries cry foul?

False accusations, hidden truths and institutional lies.

how can I not see, behind brown eyes?